WILD FOR YOU

J. C. REED

WILD FOR YOU

Copyright © 2017 J.C. Reed

All rights reserved.

Cover art by Larissa Klein

Editing by Elaine York/Allusion Graphics

ISBN: 1975936787
ISBN-13: 978-1975936785

WILD
FOR YOU

I'm an average girl.
He's a famous bull rider.
He doesn't know that I'm into him.

The first time Cash Boyd locks eyes with Erin Stone, sparks fly, and not only the clutch-at-your-sheets kind. There is something about Erin that makes him want to push her away while at the same time drives him wild for her. He's a man of many things, but being helpless at the hands of a woman isn't one of them. Finding himself at her mercy, he intends to make her job as hard as possible for her.

Burning with desire for the one man who's the shadow to her light, Erin gives in to Cash's advances...even though she could be destroyed by the truth she's afraid to disclose. Little does she know that there is also more than meets the eye to Cash and she might just get more than she bargained for.

Cash might be the best at taming bulls, but taming her heart could prove to be the greatest challenge of his life.

DEDICATION

This book is for those who never give up dreaming and believing in love. Here's to new beginnings, second chances, hot cowboys, enjoying a night under the stars, and to living in the moment.

PROLOGUE

CASH

THE CROWD RAMPS UP for action, cheering, bellowing a noisy welcome. They want me out there. Riding that bull like my life depends on it. I wink at a chick I've been eyeballing for the last ten minutes and signal the helper to get ready for me.

Riding women and bulls is my specialty.

I'm a pro at both.

I've done this a million times.

Heck, I could probably do it in my sleep.

"Hey, Cash."

I spin around at the sound of the unfamiliar voice, an easy-going grin on my lips. My eyes quickly appraise the blonde chick. She's in her early twenties and wearing a bright shade of pink lipstick. I almost expect her to start chewing bubble gum, but she doesn't. Instead, she bounces toward me, her breasts on full display in the thin tank top she probably calls a shirt.

"Hey, darlin'. You probably came to see me." Darlin' is my standard pet name. I don't bother to ask for her real name when I have no intention of remembering it.

She giggles, the sound slightly grating on my nerves. But hey, she's here and she's obviously available. And more importantly, I haven't fucked her yet, hence she's fresh meat.

"I actually came with my friends. We've been dying to see you." She's pointing to my right to a group of young women, waving. "I was hoping I'd bump into you." She wraps a long lock of hair around her finger and winks. It's beyond me why women think that's a turn on. But I play along.

I always do.

The invitation is there, hanging in the air between us. "Today's your lucky day. I'm game for more than a bit of small talk."

I grin, and she giggles. I check the time, wondering whether I could squeeze in a quickie before that bull meets his demise, and grimace. "Give me twenty minutes."

She pouts but nods her head.

I check the average on the board before I draw the bull. A rank bull named Dillinger is going to be my one last win before I'm crowned champ of the world. Dillinger is known for his dangerous temper and tendency for bucking. In the last six years and over two hundred outs, he's thrown every single rider. All fear him. Many have opted out.

But he hasn't met me yet.

I'm going to tame the beast because I was born for this.

"Cash Boyd, ladies and gentleman," the announcer says, laying out the highs and few lows of my career, then goes on to rattle down Dillinger's rap sheet.

The crowd goes wild. I grin for the cameras. The flank man's ready.

This is the moment everyone's been waiting for.

Cash Boyd—bull riding champion of the world.

A camera's angling on me from somewhere above.

I can almost taste the success as I'm readying

myself in my designated chute. I slip my palm under the handle, and pulling the rope tight, I wrap the loose tail around my hand. Adjusting my body until the handle is in the right position, I signal the gate man.

The buzzer rings.

The chute gate swings open.

The familiar rush of adrenaline flows through me.

Excitement vibrates through my body.

Eight seconds—that's how long I have to hold on.

It's all about reaction, speed, adjustment.

Show no fear.

Using my spurs to hold on to the body is the hardest part. Too far back and I'll fall. Too far forward and I'm done. Kicking his hind legs, I can tell Dillinger is one angry bull that knows how to throw.

The noise of the crowd becomes a thrumming backdrop in my mind as I cling on to Dillinger. As expected, he lunges forward, then spins wildly with a savage buck. My muscles ache from the effort of cutting with him.

For the first few seconds, I anticipate his every move, every buck, every change in direction.

I control him.

My pulse is racing in a good way.

Cash Boyd—world champ.

The bull beneath me thrashes and rears.

A few more seconds and the world champ title is mine.

But something happens. A moment of poor focus. Just when I think I've figured out his next move, the bull spins too wildly, far to the right, and my balance shifts. I lose my grip. My body doesn't register it until I land hard on my side, all the air knocked out of my lungs. The crowd gasps—or maybe it's just me.

A sharp pang shoots up my legs, and I grimace, blinded by the white-hot pain surging through me.

My first impulse is to get up, but everything is throbbing and burning.

The buzzer sounds, but it's too late.

"Cash, get the fuck away!" someone yells. Is that my brother, Kellan?

I almost turn to scan the crowd for my family when the bull lowers his horns. He's hooking for me.

The motherfucker!

Groaning, I try to clamber to my feet to get out of the way, but my legs won't carry me.

"Cash!" More people yell, their voices barely penetrating the aching fog inside my mind.

My world's spinning, and not in a good way. The bull's dashing for me. Voices shout. I think I see a rodeo clown trying to distract the beast, but I can't tell for sure because my vision's blurry and everything's spinning.

Hands wrap around my arms and shoulders, their grip rough, crushing my bones. I peer around me, realizing those aren't hands, but horns. I'm being lifted up in the air, and for a brief second, I peer straight into Dillinger's angry eyes.

The motherfucker got me.

My body's an aching pulp.

Everything's distorted.

I was so close to winning.

That's my last coherent thought before I close my eyes and succumb to the darkness, eager to escape the pain.

CHAPTER ONE

ERIN

"THIS IS THE farm," Trent Boyd says. "I don't expect you to help with the work. God knows my son will be enough of a handful. Just make sure he gets better."

I smile at the town sheriff, trying not to gawk at the sprawling estate stretching in front of us. This is no farm I've ever seen, and I've sure seen plenty of those where I grew up. The palazzo-style mansion with its carved, marble stairs leading up to the entry looks a bit out of place surrounded by trees and greenery.

I ignore the warning bells in my head at the sight of the sprawling estate, and focus back on the conversation.

"He's disgruntled by what happened. Understandably so, but deep down, if you look past his frustration, he's a good man," Trent goes on to explain. "He's just lost his faith, that's all. So, if he tells you that he doesn't need your help, please, don't listen to him, Erin. Please, don't quit."

"I won't. It can be a long and painful path to gaining full mobility. As you said it's understandable that a patient loses their faith. I'm used to that." I grant him a self-assured smile—the kind I know will infuse confidence into him, even though I know next to nothing about my new patient.

"If you need anything—" Trent hesitates as he kills the engine of his pickup truck and gets out to help me with my luggage.

"I have your number, Mr. Boyd. Don't worry. I've dealt with patients with various kinds of injuries for the last five years. I'm sure your son and I will get along just fine."

His brows draw in response. Standing in front of him, I get the chance to scrutinize him for the first time since he picked me up from the airport and drove the hundred-mile distance to Madison Creek,

Montana. Judging from his lined face, he must be in his fifties, tall, with salt and pepper hair that suits his tanned face and gives him a youthful appearance. He looks good for his age, but there's a glint of worry in his eyes.

"Please, call me Trent," he says. "You can take my son's car to drive to town. The keys are inside. Here's your expense account." He hands me a credit card, which I take with reluctance. Even after five years on the job, staying in the same house with a patient still feels strange. "The money's not just for groceries. Please, buy whatever you need. If there's anything else, whatever it is, call me and I'll be over within the hour. As much as I'd like to pretend otherwise, Cash can be insufferable. But he has a good heart. It's just this damn injury got to him, that's all. He doesn't like to feel—"

"Helpless." I nod knowingly. "Young men often don't like that feeling. Don't worry, Mr. Boyd— Trent," I add as I catch his expression. "I—"

"He's fired so many before you. We had to fly you in all the way from Chicago." He carries my luggage like it weighs nothing as we walk up the path that winds up the front lawn and drops it with a thud in front of the door. "Thousands of miles." He shakes his head grimly.

I want to know how many exactly he's fired, but refrain from asking. "I'll need your son's medical files."

"They're in your room. The equipment you requested has been set up in one of the spare rooms," Trent says and points to the door. "Well, that's as far as I'll go."

That's a strange statement. I can't help but wonder whether his son has imposed a ban on his own father who seems like such a nice man.

Then again, I've never seen a bull-riding injury before. But from what I've gathered from Trent, Cash can't move around a lot. Men in his age group, particularly the successful ones, don't take any kind of injuries too well and they tend to lash out because of it.

"I'll take it from here, thank you," I say.

"Thanks for coming," Trent says for the umpteenth time, his warm tone brimming with gratitude.

I reward him with my most reassuring smile and wave at him as I watch him drive off to the sound of screeching tires and the smell of whirled-up dust.

Dragging my suitcase behind me, I try the door and to my surprise, find it unlocked. Living in Chicago, unlocked doors, vast pastures, and a country house the size of a mansion isn't what I'm used to. Even the weather seems to smile down on me. I've never been to Montana but I can already tell it's going to be a beautiful few months. So what if the house owner's said to be a bit cranky?

I drag my suitcase through the open door and slam it behind me.

The house is eerily silent. I'm standing in a generously sized hall, which stretches into a vast living area with wood beams and a fresco-painted, coffered ceiling. The furnishing is modern—plush white sofas that lack the female touch of cushions and comfy throws.

I instantly feel at home, and I'm already seeing myself filling vases with the wildflowers growing all around the black iron wrought-iron fence.

Flowers are good for the soul and a great aid in speeding up a client's recovery.

I leave my suitcase in the hall and breeze from room to room to familiarize myself with my surroundings. A smaller, more casual living room opens into a generous and perfectly trimmed backyard. The massive kitchen is outfitted with marble countertops and dark wood cabinetry, and offers a stunning view of the mountains stretching in the distance. Right next to the library stuffed with bookcases and books are two doors, one ajar and one closed. I peek through the open door and find a bedroom dominated by a large, four-poster bed. On top of the spread are fresh towels, a thin folder containing medical files, and an envelope addressed to "the new girl."

Leaving my suitcase in the doorway, I sit down on the bed and pull a note out of the envelope.

Hey,

As you can see, I'm not addressing you by your name because I haven't bothered asking about it. The thing is, I didn't employ you, and I most certainly don't need your help. You probably want to be in Montana just as much as I want you here. So, let's cut this charade short and say goodbye before we've even met. I'm enclosing a parting gift in the sum of five hundred bucks, which should cover your plane ticket back home.

Best wishes,

Cash Boyd

P.S.: In case you're thinking of sticking around, get out of my way. Make me breakfast, if you must.

But never knock on my bedroom door, don't talk to me if you see me, and get the hell out of my way. And never talk about God, because I won't join your cult.

Is this a fucking joke?

Frowning, I fold the note and slowly push it back inside the envelope.

I've just unofficially met Cash Boyd. It might only be on paper, but I think my first impression of him is a pretty solid one.

Injured or not, depressed or not, the guy's a jerk with a capital J. His dad's description of him probably did him justice.

But there's also a glimmer of hope...he has a sense of humor.

I have a reputation of being good at what I do, which is probably why Trent Boyd offered me good money to accompany his son on his way to recovery. As a professional, I pride myself in my ability to keep my cool at all times, which is why the note doesn't deter me from my mission one bit.

I take my time unpacking, stacking my clothes and few belongings neatly in the walk-in closet. I keep my shower short, mostly because I can't wait to explore the place that will be my home for the next few months. I pile my hair up before I shrug into my work attire—black slacks and a white shirt—all comfortable to work in but not that I look like I'm about to spend a quiet evening on the couch, watching whatever's on cable.

It's late afternoon when I head out of my bedroom in search of Cash Boyd.

CHAPTER TWO

CASH

THERE'S A PLACE in a man's life that's reserved just for him. It's his cave. His one true love. The one place he'll go to when everything else falls to pieces.

Visit Club 69...we know how to take care of you.

I frown at the new slogan my PA has just emailed me. It's about the biggest bullshit I've ever heard, but I'm in the bullshit business and know how to sell it well. Club 69 has become a brand, and I'm the main attraction. My picture's in the media all the time. Whatever I endorse, sells. But right now, I can't even promote the new club I'm about to open because of a tiny inconvenience.

I wince as I push to my feet, unsure how to balance my weight. The cast I'm wearing has been an inconvenience, to say the least. But more so it's been a hindrance. I can't turn up at my own club shuffling on crutches and ruin the reputation I've worked my ass off to build. So, I have to rely on my most-trusted employees to ensure my business stays ahead of the competition.

I speed-dial my PA, Amanda, and bark into the phone, "The slogan's crap. Arrange a video chat with the branding department first thing tomorrow morning." With that, I hang up.

Amanda will know what to do. She's been with me right from the beginning, when I was just a cowboy with big aspirations and a hundred grand borrowed from his rock star brother. Kellan left the big business behind to settle for the quiet life Montana has to offer. I decided to leave Montana behind for the glitzy life my string of clubs has to offer.

All was well...until that bull threw me off and ruined my life.

Shuffling out of my office, I head for the kitchen at the pace of a snail. I see her before she sees me. She's leaning against the doorframe, her hand gingerly clasped around the doorknob, black pants hugging the curves of her tight little ass as she peers into one of the guestrooms. Her delicate neck is exposed—all milky skin that's begging to be held down as you ride her.

From behind, she looks tiny, but there's something in her determined stance that instantly tells me she's not like the others my annoying family has hired so far. That would worry me under usual circumstances, but all I can do is stare at that ass of hers, mentally undressing it.

My dick jumps to life, eager to get some much-needed action.

I've no idea who she is, just that my meddling family must have hired a new physical therapist.

I can't help but stare. Damn, it's been too long since I've caught a glimpse of someone like her.

This leg injury has been more than an inconvenience. In the months since the accident, I've barely left the house to get fresh air, let alone go in search of my next conquest. It sure helped that my past therapists weren't exactly fuckable.

I don't know if I should thank my father for

practically serving a pretty little thing to me on a silver platter, or stop taking his calls for the next two years.

I try to turn away before she can spy me, but it's too late.

Closing the door, she spins on her heels, and our eyes connect. They're blue and wide and sparkle with the kind of intelligence I don't usually go for in a woman. For a moment, there's confusion written on her face, which is quickly succeeded by scorn as she brushes her brown hair out of her eyes and takes a step forward.

Ah, she didn't take too kindly to my little note, which was supposed to be part joke, part scare off tactic.

"Mr. Boyd? I'm Erin Stone, your new physical therapist."

She inches toward me, the soles of her flat sandals slapping against the tile floor. She's moving with the agility of someone who knows how to use her body, but it's her eyes that have my heart beating just a little bit faster.

I attribute it to the sudden blood flow to the lower parts of my body.

"I see you didn't get the memo." I cross my arms over my chest, ignoring the tightness in my pants.

"Actually, I did, but I've never been one to follow orders, which apparently you like to give, Mr. Boyd." She takes another step forward. Her head is thrown back so she can look all the way up. She should be unsettled by my height, and yet all I can find in her eyes is more determination. "You shouldn't have wasted your breath writing the note you left on my bed because I'm not your employee. You don't know me. You don't get to tell me what to do. And you most certainly won't intimidate me by being a jerk. I've seen bigger." Maybe it's my imagination, but I swear her glance brushes the front of my pants, hovering there for a moment too long. Her tongue flicks across her lower lip.

I want to bite that lip. I want to draw it between my teeth while I entangle my hands in her hair. I want to pull her head back, leaving her to my mercy, as I run my tongue over her soft skin, making her quiver for more.

But I do none of those things. Instead, I regard her with the kind of arrogance I've reserved for pretty much everyone who's been trying to tell me what to do the last few months.

"Everyone knows that size is only a number. It's what you make of it that counts. I can offer both. Now, please, go away." I shoot her another cold gaze and hop down the hall into my office as fast as my crutches and the pain in my leg and hip will allow me, leaving her staring after me.

That shut her right up.

As I slam the door, I realize I never even asked to see her résumé. She could be a criminal who's benefitting from an unlocked front door and the fact that everyone in town knows I go through therapists like some people go through underwear.

Wouldn't that be a nice change in an otherwise dull day?

The thought brings a smile to my face. The first in months.

I plop down on the sofa with a cuss word lodged in my throat.

Fuck, it's been months and my leg's still hurting like a bitch.

Right after the fall I lost consciousness and can't remember anything. But I've watched the video over and over again. What that bull did to me wasn't a pretty sight. I still cringe whenever I watch his horns lift me up and toss me through the air like a rag doll, a moment before people rush to distract the bull.

I boot up my laptop and replay the video for the umpteenth time. My face is in full view, bruised and bloodied; my body is motionless, the leg bent at an unnatural angle. If it wasn't me in the video, I'd think the guy was dead.

It's frightening to see, and that's not a feeling I'm accustomed to, which is what's kept me angry ever since I made it out of the hospital and Kellan let me watch my last performance.

He shouldn't have...because scrutinizing myself over and over again is pretty much all I can do all day long, if only to torture myself for the stupid mistake I made.

Even a rookie would have known better than to spend the previous night with some meaningless chick rather than get the sleep that would have turned me into the bull riding world champ I should be.

If I had stayed in my hotel room like Kellan and Ryder instructed, I wouldn't have lost focus. I would be back in Las Vegas or NYC or Chicago, back in business, back doing what I'm known for.

Manage my famous Club 69 empire and earn big bucks.

The knowledge stings, but what stings even more is the reproach and worry I keep seeing in my family's eyes.

"Cash Boyd, the family's screw-up," I mumble and close the video, ready to get back to work, if only to forget my father's words for a few hours.

But words aren't forgotten easily. And so they keep lingering at the back of my mind as I go through the rows of numbers on the spreadsheets, matching up expenses and profits.

I may be a screw-up, but at least I'm the kind who knows how to turn it into serious money.

CHAPTER THREE

ERIN

ACCORDING TO MY file, Cash Boyd is twenty-eight years old and was in perfect health up until his accident, which left his shoulder and hip dislocated, his collarbone shattered, and the bones in his right leg broken in several places. He spent a few weeks in a hospital, undergoing three surgeries that left him in pain but with excellent prospects of making a full recovery.

The swelling retreated quickly, but with no physical therapy, he's made no progress.

That doesn't come as a surprise. Given his age and the hostility he showed earlier today, it looks like he's someone who's accustomed to always having his own way. I've seen it before. I've worked with patients like him. He's rejecting everyone's help because he thinks he can do it alone, on his own terms.

In this respect, he's stubborn as a mule.

The trouble is, the more time passes, the harder it gets to regain full mobility.

"How's the new job?" Debra asks.

"Fine." My voice sounds a bit too high-pitched as I sit down on my bed, cradling my phone between my chin and my shoulder blade.

The truth is, Cash Boyd in real life is even worse than on paper. If I don't change the subject soon, Debra will pick up on it. The last thing I want is to admit to my sister that she was right when she warned me not to take this job. "The house is great. And the weather's great."

"How's your new patient?"

I cringe.

Of course.

She *had* to ask.

How to describe Cash Boyd in words that don't include 'jerk,' 'jackass,' and 'arrogant prick?'

And definitely leave out 'fuck, he's hot.'

"I think he's a hermit. Very private." I settle against the pillows and tuck my legs beneath me, unsure whether to smile or groan at the realization that that's not the only thing Cash Boyd is.

Cash Boyd is more like the kind of eye candy you invite into your bed to fuck your brains out. And then you tell him to chuck his phone number into the nearest dumpster because guys like him aren't called 'heartbreakers' for no reason.

Trust me, been there, done that.

Never again.

"Oh? In what way?" Debra's voice betrays none of her emotions, which is a sure sign that she's listening intently, ready to make up her own mind and judge the hell out of you if you reveal too much.

"Well." I tuck a strand of hair behind my ear as I choose my words carefully. "He's not exactly the kind who wants the help of a therapist. The next few months will be a bit challenging. But don't worry. I know what I'm doing. This is going to look great on my résumé. And I need the money."

Not to mention the thousands of air miles between Chicago and Montana.

"Erin." Heavy pause. Thick waves of tension carry down the phone line, bringing with them all the guilt, accusation, and turmoil I thought I had left behind back home.

"I'm fine," I whisper and draw a silent breath, wondering whether my statement could be further from the truth.

"Are you sure?"

"Yes." Another sharp breath.

I can do this. Madison Creek is the right place for it. No one knows me here; no one will try to dig up my story.

"Okay." Debra's voice betrays her doubt. If I were back home, she wouldn't let me off the hook so easily. But thousands of miles, even for her, is too big of a distance to keep being pushy. We both know it. "You'll call if you need anything?"

"Yes," I say, even though that's a lie, too. Debra has her own family and set of problems. I could never add to her plate.

"Anything at all, Erin. I mean it. That's what sisters are for."

She says her goodbye. I breathe a sigh of relief as we disconnect. I have no answers for her questions because I have no answers for myself.

I close my eyes and rest for a while, my cell

pressed against my chest. It's late evening when I make my way downstairs, expecting the kitchen to be empty.

"I thought you were gone." The low husk of Cash's voice startles me.

I press a hand against my chest and look up into his impossibly green eyes, expecting to find anger, challenge, anything but—

Indifference.

His gaze is so cold it freezes me to the core.

"I—"

I shiver involuntarily as my mind goes blank from the sudden onset of guilt.

What's there to feel guilty about?

I may be unwanted, but I'm not an intruder.

It's a job. I'm being paid to help. He should be thankful for that, and yet he acts as though I'm the last person he wants around.

"Believe it or not, you are my responsibility, and I take my responsibilities very seriously." I raise my chin defiantly, which seems to slowly become a pattern around him. "Your father hired me, meaning I'll leave when he asks me to."

"Is that so?" His mouth sets and his gaze brushes over me, moving from head to toe, though not in that lingering kind of way.

He's assessing me as though this is a job interview.

I try to remember what he does when he's not risking his life riding bulls, but can't remember.

Dammit!

I should have Googled him, find out the kind of person he is before I accepted this job. But the last few months weren't exactly kind to me.

"Maybe I don't look like much, but I'm one of the best at what I do."

"What is it that you do—what did you say your name was?" He leans into the kitchen counter and crosses his arms over his broad chest, his muscles rippling beneath his shirt, straining the seams. There's a gleam of pain in his eyes, which he hides just as quickly as it appeared.

Under usual circumstances, I would show sympathy. But not today.

The guy couldn't even be bothered to remember my name!

"I'm your new physical therapist." I emphasize the last word just in case he thinks I'm the help or something. And if he wants to know my name he'll have to ask again.

"So, you're the one who'll rub my back and tuck me into bed at night." His cold glare breaks in favor of a leering smile. "I bet that's not all you're good at."

Now we've entered familiar territory.

What is it with guys and the sexual innuendoes when they confuse my job description with someone who works in a massage parlor?

"I'm here to help you get back on your feet, not get you off, Mr. Boyd. There definitely won't be any happy endings. Bedwise, that is."

His lips twitch. "Bedwise? Is that even a word?"

"It is now." My eyes throw daggers. Unfortunately, it doesn't seem to have any effect on his stupid grin. "If you're looking for a hooker, I'll be happy to call one for you. Should you try anything—"

"Relax, sweetheart," Cash says, cutting me off. "I don't ever impose on a woman. They usually impose on me."

Looking at him, I can imagine why.

His deep laughter travels through my abdomen, leaving a tight sensation behind.

"I'm glad we've established that," I say a bit too breathily. "We'll be starting tomorrow. Eight a.m. sharp. Make sure to wear something comfortable. I'm fair but hard, and have no doubt that I'll get you back to your old self in an appropriate amount of time."

His brows shoot up, and his eyes twinkle with amusement. "I can't wait to find out what your hands are capable of."

I don't know why his words make me blush. Maybe it's the glint in his eyes or the leery look— whatever it is, I feel unhinged in a strange way, as though someone very sexy has just whispered into my ear all the things he'd like to do to me tonight.

"You know what, make it seven a.m.," I mumble and get out without so much as a glance over my shoulder.

But I can hear him mumble something like, "I'm usually up at six."

***

Once I'm back in my room, I make sure to lock the door and drop onto my bed, burying my head in the lavender-scented pillows.

What have I gotten myself into?

Cash Boyd is easily the hottest guy I've ever met.

He's tall with a body chiseled in pure perfection. His green eyes are devoid of emotion but shimmer with intelligence, as though everything he says and does is part of a carefully planned agenda.

His huge home and upscale furnishing scream money. I'm not naïve enough to think he's just a stupid bull rider with no brains and no aspirations. But I'm also not foolish enough to want to know more about him or his personal life.

Instead of Googling him, I pull out his medical file to have another peek at it as I prepare my therapy plan and munch on the spare chocolate bar I always carry in my handbag.

I refuse to let his pure, raw sexiness stop me from doing my job.

I refuse to become weak.

The sooner I've gotten him to the point where he can walk without those crutches, the sooner I can leave and forget him.

That's the plan, and I never deviate from my plans.

CHAPTER FOUR

CASH

IT'S EARLY MORNING when I head into the kitchen. Last night's encounter with my new physical therapist has left me in a strangely good mood. There's something about her eyes and the stubbornness displayed in them that amuses me.

It's been so long since a woman's challenged me the way she does.

I'm not used to women taking charge. At least not outside of the bedroom.

And then there's also the fact that she's crazy

attractive. It's been too long since I've actually had to chase a woman.

Too long since I felt the buzz, the thrill of the chase, the satisfaction that comes with conquering her. Whatever this is, it's a nice change from my usual routine.

She didn't like the memo, but her reaction to it was surprisingly calm. It was supposed to drive her away. That she's decided to stay and put up with me is baffling.

When the door swings open, I turn around to regard her with a fake scowl on my face.

"Good morning to you, too, Mr. Boyd." She frowns when I say nothing.

What's with the Mr. Boyd stuff?

I'm still watching her as she walks past me to get to the sink. She's dressed in the same boring attire as last night, but in the light of day she looks even more fragile. Usually, I don't pay attention to such banalities, but her haunted look stops me from appreciating the generous swell of her breasts clearly contoured beneath her matronly top.

"Coffee?" I point to the coffee maker.

"No, thank you. I was just getting a cup of tea," she mumbles, avoiding my roaming gaze. I notice the box she's carrying in her hand and raise my brows, waiting for her to explain.

Ignoring me, she goes on to boil water. But her tense shoulders reveal her nervousness around me.

Or maybe she's still pissed.

"You brought along your own tea?" I ask.

"It's a special blend."

"What is it? Tea that promises your clients will walk over water?"

She turns around, and the defiant glint from last night is back in her eyes. "No, it's just green tea. Organic. From protected forests." She leans forward, leaning against the counter, and I can't help but throw a fleeting look at her breasts. "Did you know that harvesting tea often involves child labor and slavery?"

"No, but enlighten me," I say sarcastically.

"You're not interested in hearing more?"

I shrug. "You want me to care what happened out there while I was in a wheelchair? While I could still end up in a wheelchair? I'm sorry, but I don't give a fuck." Silence fills the air, and I realize that my comment was a bit harsh. Of course, I care what happens in the world, which is why I support several charities. I just don't need to be reminded that the world's one fucked-up place in general.

"You want some?" I ask and take a bite of my ham

and cheese sandwich, my gaze brushing over her disheveled hair and the flash of nerves flickering in her blue eyes.

"No, thank you."

"You don't eat?" Without waiting for her reply I push a sandwich toward her and watch as she gazes at it longingly. Our brief interaction last night had her running for her bedroom, meaning she probably skipped dinner. I feel bad, but on the other hand I can't be friendly to her or else she'll want to hang around to 'help' me.

I don't need anyone's help.

"I'm fine," she mumbles.

"Come on. Take a bite. I promise it's not poisoned." My comment doesn't garner me the smile or giggle I expected.

I expect her to decline again, when she grabs the sandwich and takes a ginger bite, chewing slowly.

She really wants this to work out.

That has to be the only reasonable explanation why she's not leaving.

Or she needs the money. Desperately.

Taking a sip of my coffee, I realize I can't remember whether she told me her name last night. For some reason, it bugs me just as much as the fact that my sexual innuendo didn't render the response

I would have expected. Instead of melting her panties, it just made her turn a few degrees colder in the blink of an eye.

"Care to introduce yourself since you seem keen on living in my house?" I raise a brow and cock a smile. But she doesn't seem to get my attempt at infusing humor into the situation.

"I'm not keen on living in your house at all." She puts her sandwich down on the counter and her back goes rigid, pushing her breasts into focus. "It's my job to be here, with my patient."

"Why are you doing it? Staying, I mean. There are plenty of other clients to choose from." I deliberately use the word 'client' not 'patient.'

"The greatest reward for me is to see progress in my patients." She emphasizes the last word.

"Do I happen to be a challenge for you?"

Her gaze meets mine with a force I never thought I'd find in a woman. "Yes. If you put it that way, absolutely."

I can't help staring at them...her breasts. How would they feel in my hands? I might not get much action these days, but I'm a man, after all. And I'm not blind. They look amazing in spite of the baggy shirt she's wearing.

"How many patients have you helped to walk?" I

ask, barely able to pry my gaze off her chest.

"Are you asking me for my progress chart?"

"If you have it laying around, that'd be great. I'd love to have a look at it." Among other things.

She turns her back to me again as she pours hot water into a cup. "You'd be my twenty-sixth patient."

"So few?" I raise my brows in mock ridicule.

"Who've learned to walk again." She throws me a cold glance. "Do you have any idea how much time I put into my job, Mr. Boyd? I'm asking because you're sending out the distinct message that you think I'm not taking this seriously."

"I'll pay you good money to leave."

She cocks her head to the side. "Don't do that. I'm not going home, not before I've seen you walk. And I promise you will one day. Even if I have to force you, I will." Her tone is resolute. She probably believes her own promise. I wish I could say the same about me.

"I still don't know your name. I'm not sure I feel comfortable with a stranger living in my house," I say, eager to change the subject.

"I tried to introduce myself and you brushed me off, Mr. Boyd." She pushes her hair back.

I smirk.

Little Miss Prissy thinks she can talk back.

Fat chance.

When I ask a question, I demand an answer;

I always *get* an answer.

It's as simple as that.

"Okay." I shrug. "Then let's call you 'sunshine.'"

"I'm not your sunshine."

"Thunder, perhaps?"

"Absolutely not." Her eyes narrow and a glint of anger flashes in them. "It's Erin."

"You don't look like an Erin."

"No? What do I look like?"

She has a short fuse. I can't help but wonder whether she's as fiery in bed as she is outside of it.

The thought sends a rush of blood to my dick. My jeans tighten visibly. But even if I wanted to hide the bulge, the cast around my leg makes it impossible to shift position.

"Birdy." I press my mouth into a tight line to suppress a grin.

"Don't call me that." Her voice is sharp, on edge. Flashes of anger flicker in her eyes. She looks as though she's about to snap my head off, which turns me on even more.

"Why not? Don't you like the word, the implication of it, or is it reserved for someone else?"

"I—" Her gaze darts around the kitchen as she

struggles for words. Her expression is cagey, but her emotions are written all over her face. "Because it used to be my nickname."

"Birdy?"

"Yeah, I don't want you to call me that. Ever. It's Erin. Please."

Her blue eyes fill with moisture. She turns her head away, but not in time to hide the pain that pours from her.

"If you don't mind, I'd like to start our first session. I'll prepare the guestroom," she mumbles.

"I like the sound of that. You'll find fresh linens in the cupboard in the hall."

"You may call that flirting; I call it sexual harassment. Now, drink up your coffee. We're beginning in ten."

"Ten what?"

"Minutes, Mr. Boyd." She exhales a long, exasperated breath that makes her chest heave. I smile, unable to help myself.

"What if I'm not ready by then?"

"Then we'll be having a problem," Erin says. "Your father—"

"—is paying you. Got it the first couple of times you mentioned it. He's paying you to put up with my shit."

"Good. Now that that's sorted out, let's begin." She's not even trying to pretend otherwise. Turning sharply on her heels, she heads for the door, calling over her shoulder, "We'll do it in the living room, then."

"You realize the words 'We'll do it' are sending mixed messages, right? You may think I'm flirting, but I call it working with what you're giving me. I would be careful how you talk to your patients. Or else—"

She spins back to me, her eyes two fiery pits. "Or else?"

I open my mouth to proclaim that I don't mind the living room because I have a very comfortable sofa that's suitable for any position she might desire. But something stops me. Clearly, she's not the flirty kind. Or she's not over the breakup of her last relationship. Whatever it is, there's something about her that suddenly kills my mood to further wind her up.

"Or nothing." I push the remnants of my sandwich into my mouth and chew slowly, wondering why the fuck I even care about her feelings.

What the hell?

She might not be the type I usually go for, but no

woman is ever off-limits... considering the circumstances. The circumstances being the three, five-hour surgeries I had to endure, followed by the steel implant in my bone, then the cast on my foot rendering me glued to this house for months.

Her glance remains fixed on me for a second too long. Without another word, she turns around and leaves.

But I caught the fleeting glance.

I know that sparkle in her eyes.

The longing. The passion. The hunger.

She's actually attracted to me.

She knows the impact my accident had on my sex life, and she's still attracted.

It's not like I haven't been horny. My right hand hasn't seen so much action since high school. But I can't call any of the numbers stored in my phone. Madison Creek is my home—my private retreat from my hectic lifestyle back in Chicago.

None of my conquests have ever seen the inside of this house, and that's exactly the way I'd like to keep it. I don't need anyone invading my private space—neither a woman, nor the media.

I won't let the paparazzi enter my real life to get to know the real me.

And there's also the fact that I'm not comfortable

with the world knowing how hard the accident really hit me. It looked bad enough on screen. But the reality is much worse.

There are days when only prescribed painkillers could make the pain bearable, but I refuse to take them. I never did in the past, and I'm not about to start now. It's a matter of regaining some of the control I used to have over my life.

The bottle of pills on my nightstand used to remind me of what I'd lost every hour of every day—before I tossed them in the bin. Erin's presence has a similar effect on me, which is why she has to leave.

Only if she weren't...

"So damn hot," I mumble. She's literally a few doors down, and the tightness in my pants just won't let me forget it.

Not that I'm planning to invite her into my bed. As things stand, it's all pretty much a diversion to waste my days...until I can get back on that bull again.

In spite of the banter we've been having I'm not going to deviate from my plan to make her stay unbearable for her.

The plan is to push her buttons as much as I can. Making her leave shouldn't be too hard. We've barely spent ten minutes together and I already have her fuming. It's only a matter of time before she snaps.

This is going to be easy.

My property's big enough to avoid her for a week. Ignoring the pain, I enter my office through the glass sliding door overlooking a spot of the backyard that is hidden from view from the living room. Even if Erin comes looking for me, I'm pretty sure she won't be taking a stroll outside through the bushes. They all think I'm useless on crutches, which is why my father and annoying brother, Kellan, keep sending people to look after me. She might be a professional, but she's just like the rest who think I can't regain the movement in my leg on my own.

CHAPTER FIVE

ERIN

MY GEAR'S SET up in the living room—two sports balls, a few colourful bands, and fluffy towels. It may not sound like much, but that's all I'll need to get Cash's muscles working. And from the looks of it, there's plenty of those to work with. After his comments, I've decided to steer clear of the guestroom and the fancy equipment before he gets the wrong idea.

I'm waiting on the soft leather sofa; my fingers tapping impatiently on my thigh.

Cash was supposed to join me forty-seven minutes ago. Either he's taking really long in the bathroom or he's decided to stand me up.

For the sake of our professional relationship, I hope it's not the latter.

A grown-up can't possibly be so defiant and rude.

Sighing, I get up and head for his bedroom, then press my ear against the closed door to listen.

No sounds.

Has he gone back to bed?

I crack the door open, almost expecting his full wrath combined with plenty of shouting to get out of his room. But he's not here. The room looks tidy, the bed's made—which is so unlike every man I've ever met. And in particular, one who can barely move.

So, where is he?

A guy limping on crutches can't get very far.

I search each room, not skipping the bathroom, then head outside.

He's on the porch, sprawled on a sun lounger. A hat is drawn on his face and casts a dark shadow on his midday stubble, and I can't help but wonder whether he skipped shaving last night and this morning.

He's changed out of his jeans into a pair of black shorts that are pulled a little lower than necessary.

His abdomen is all rows of hard muscles and smooth, tanned skin. No sign of a shirt. For a guy who can't lift weights in his current state, he's in great shape.

Scratch that.

His muscles are in perfect shape. I appreciate that as a professional who'll have to work with those muscles.

As a woman—

My mouth goes dry as I gaze past his broad chest to the happy trail leading to a perfect V. A hint of dark hair spreads down to the generous bulge in his shorts. Every single inch of his skin looks as though it's been carved from perfection. I'm tempted to trail my finger down his hard abdomen to find out whether he'd shiver under the soft touch.

But I don't.

Neither in my fantasies, nor in my dreams. And particularly not now, during working hours.

I'll reserve this delicious image for much later, once I get the job done.

Which I intend to do...with or without his cooperation.

I inch closer, making sure to make myself heard. He doesn't stir.

Is he really sleeping? Or plain ignoring me?

Frowning, I touch his shoulder, avoiding gawking at the rows of rippling muscles adorning his abdomen or the generous bulge that seems to fascinate me way more than it should.

With lightning speed, Cash's hand goes around my wrist and I topple forward onto the lounger, right on top of him. His other hand circles around my back, pushing me gently into him.

His good leg lifts up to part mine. His sun-kissed skin is hot against mine. His face is inches away from me, his green eyes shimmering with lust. I open my mouth to protest, but he's holding me so close he's squeezing all the air out of me.

My brain screams at me to jump up, put some professional distance between us. But all I can do is stare into those hypnotic eyes, my anger growing at the irritating grin on his face.

Or maybe I'm angry at the fact that my nipples are straining against the fabric of my bra, eager to spill into his willing hands. My core pulses to life as waves of want shoot through veins, reacting to his masculinity.

How can someone with a cast on his foot move so fast?

And most importantly, what the hell is he doing to me?

"You could have pulled a muscle." I try to scramble to my feet, but his grip tightens, keeping me glued to his chest.

"Sorry, reflex," Cash says, his hot breath caressing my lips.

"Nice attempt." I turn away sharply before my labored breathing can betray the effect he's having on my body. My gaze settles on his hand gripping my wrist, and I narrow my eyes in the hope he'll get the message.

"No, really." He lets go off my hand, then goes on to turn on top of me in order to push up to his feet, taking all the time in the world. Well, more like stumbles up while making sure at some point his entire body is pressed into me, his weight keeping me glued in place.

It feels so good I almost forget to breathe.

All my senses are heightened, enjoying the moment, trying to prolong it. I bite my lip hard to regain my composure, but it's not doing the trick.

Cash doesn't try to show it, but I can tell his leg's hurting him. In spite his discomfort, I feel the bulge between my legs, pressed into me, and something stirs in my abdomen.

My mouth goes dry, and all my lady parts clench in anticipation of his next move.

You did it on purpose, I want to say, and yet I keep staring at him, my mushy brain rendered useless. His mouth is so close I can feel his hot breath on my lips. Heat swirls through my body, creating an exquisite ache that begs for his touch.

A part of me wishes he'd just put some distance between us before he realizes that I want him...badly. And then there's the tiny voice in my head that tells me to make a move and go for it because, clearly, Cash isn't adverse to the idea, either. I've had my fair share of groping. It comes with the job description, and I've always warded it off without paying it much attention.

Until now.

With Cash it's different. It doesn't feel like groping.

It doesn't feel like he's mistaking my professional touch for affection. It also doesn't feel like he's trying to prove to himself that he still has what it takes to attract women.

It feels like he's into me for the sake of me, and under different circumstances I'd probably allow myself to explore this crazy sexual attraction—

I shake my head.

Don't even go there.

At last, with a low, sexy groan, Cash presses his

hand into the lounger, inches from my hip, and straightens to his feet, his eyes lingering on me.

The bit of distance he's just put between us is enough for my brain to regain its marbles.

"What did you do that for?" I ask breathily.

"Sorry. It was an honest mistake." Cash winks, the gesture betraying his real intentions.

"And you expect me to believe that?" I cross my arms over my chest, mostly to cover the tell-tale signs of my arousal. "Mr. Boyd, I'm not your hooker. I'm your physical therapist, in case you still didn't get the message. If you need someone to take care of your private needs, I'll be happy to call the appropriate number. But the stunt you just pulled is dangerous. You could have torn a muscle, or worse."

"I'm always careful," Cash mumbles.

I sigh, ignoring the sudden need to roll my eyes. "I bet you said the same thing before you fell off that bull."

I'm not usually one to dish out low blows, but someone needed to give this guy a wakeup call.

In the many years I've been working as a physical therapist, I've never encountered anyone so full of himself.

No one's ever affected me this much, either.

"It was a mistake, Erin." His hand reaches out to

touch me. Startled, I jump up, my shoulder bumping into his hard chest.

"I thought you were supposed to help me get better, not knock me over and land me in a wheelchair," Cash says with a smirk.

His voice is low and lined with gravity. Given that he's not even budged from the spot, his statement is absolutely ridiculous.

"You should have thought about that before you pulled me on top of you." I shake my head. "What are you doing out here, anyway? You kept me waiting for almost one hour." My gaze rakes over his muscular body. Taking a step to the side, I try to infuse more anger into my voice, but all that comes out of my mouth is some raspy breathing that sounds suspiciously like I'm fazed by his proximity and near-nakedness.

Which I'm not, obviously.

I just wish he'd put some damn clothes on, that's all.

"I can see right through you. You're not as unaffected as you're pretending to be." The double meaning is there, hanging heavy in the air. His brows are drawn and his lips are twitching, as though whatever's going on in his dirty mind is the joke of the year.

"I'm most certainly not affected by a great body and a bit of naked skin. I'm more bothered by the fact that you think it's okay to lie around half naked." The words leave my mouth before I can stop myself. I sound so defensive, I could crawl under a rock and die from sheer mortification.

"I wasn't thinking along those lines, but now that you mentioned it. I had no idea you'd be bothered by the fact that I'm trying to relax in my *own* home." His magnificent lips curl into a languid smile and my stomach sinks a little.

He looked gorgeous in that kitchen last night and this morning. But in the bright light, he's stunning.

Sexy without even trying.

And everything I've vowed to steer clear of.

"You call that relaxing?"

"Okay. I'll admit, I was hiding from you."

His fingers graze the side of my face, as though to brush back my hair, but no breeze is blowing.

"I'm not your enemy, Mr. Body." My mouth clamps shut at the realization I've just made a huge blunder.

Crap.

He is Mr. Body, alright, but he doesn't need to hear that from me. His sudden grin speaks volumes. Gathering every ounce of strength I have, I add frostily, "Mr. Boyd."

His brows shoot up. "Yes?"

"You still remember I'm here for work purposes, right?"

"Of course. I don't suffer from dementia. Or Alzheimer's. Luckily."

"Funny." I smirk. "Now that we've clarified that part, I'm asking you to get ready for a little workout."

The tip of his tongue flicks over his lips. I know what he's thinking; I can see it in his hooded eyes and feel it in the electric current passing through his fingers into me.

You can't blame a guy for being horny, and certainly not when he's probably been shacked up in his house for way longer than he ever imagined.

"What did you have in mind?" His hand reaches up, probably to brush that imaginary strand of hair away from my face again.

Hell to the no.

I swat at his hand and turn on my heels, calling over my shoulder, "Please, let me do my work so you can start doing yours. I expect you to join me in the living room in five minutes, Mr. Boyd."

With that, I head back inside, ignoring the low chuckle I'm pretty sure was for my benefit.

Once inside, I sit back down on the sofa, prepared to wait out the five minutes before I head back out to drag him to his first physical therapy session, if need be.

Mr. Body.

What the hell was I thinking?

This is going to come back to bite me for the rest of my stay.

***

An hour later, I'm still sitting on the sofa, wondering why I'm even putting up with Cash Boyd rather than packing my bags and leaving.

My patients get angry with me.

They yell. They sometimes cry. But no one stands me up. Ever. Because, inside they all want to get better.

But you can't shove your help down someone's throat if they don't want it. That's a fact. Cash Boyd seems to fall into the kind of category I haven't met yet: the kind who can't wait to get rid of me.

The kind who prefers to wallow and drown in self pity.

Pulling out my phone, I type up a quick text message to my sister to tell her that I'm fine. Taking a mental step back is a way to stop myself from packing up my therapy gear. I want to leave so badly, I almost dial the airport to inquire about the next flight back home.

But something holds me back.

I'm not wanted here; I get that. Trent warned me. I expected it, but somehow, I hadn't realized how difficult his son could really be.

And so damn hot!

It's not just his unwillingness to work with me. It's also his damn remarks and the fact that I'm actually enjoying the way his eyes seem to drink in my body. I'm used to getting lewd remarks every now and then, but they never affected me in any way.

Until now.

"That's ridiculous," I mumble to myself. "He's just a guy."

A hot one, I'll admit, but a man, nonetheless.

By taking on this job, Cash Boyd has become my responsibility, not least because I made a promise to his father. And strangely, for some reason, unknown to me, I want to help him, which is why I'll have to get a grip on this ridiculous attraction I feel toward him.

"Mr. Boyd!" I yell even though I know better than

to expect an answer. My voice reverberates off the walls and—

Nothing.

"Mr. Boyd," I yell again, this time louder. My voice echoes back at me, cementing the fact that I'm alone.

Still no answer.

Annoyed as hell, I head outside. He's no longer on the porch. No sight of him whatsoever. It's a huge house, so it comes as no surprise that I didn't hear him go back inside.

Sighing, I decide to go for a walk to cool my head off.

No point of running after Cash Boyd if he's in the mood to run from me.

Maybe he'll give this a chance later when he's come to his senses.

CHAPTER SIX

ERIN

WHEN I RETURN from my walk, there's still no sign of Cash. No note. Not even the faint scent of his aftershave. It's like he was never here this morning. I'm about to pour myself another cup of tea when the door swings open.

"Mr. Boyd. I'm glad you've decided to—" Frowning, I turn around sharply and stare at the woman. She's in her sixties with gray, curly hair that keeps falling into her face. She's cradling two brown bags full of groceries that look too heavy for her small frame.

"I hope I didn't startle you. You must be Erin?"

"I am."

"I'm Margaret. I'm helping with the household."

Of course, the guy has a housekeeper.

An estate as big as this must take a lot of time and work to maintain. And then there's also the fact that someone must be cooking the stocked-up meals in the refrigerator.

I hurry to take the bags from her and place them on the counter. "Nice to meet you."

She nods a thank-you. "Trent has told me so much about you. We were all so excited when you agreed to help Cash. How do you like it here?"

"It's great." I'm not even lying. I do like Montana, the country life, the house...maybe not so much its owner. "I have yet to get used to how quiet it is compared to Chicago."

She lets out a laugh, and we proceed to unpack the groceries, and restock the fridge.

"I've just made myself a cup of tea. Would you like some?" I offer once we're done. I refrain from mentioning my special blend.

"Sure." She takes a seat at the table and folds her hands in her lap. As I pour the lukewarm tea into two mugs, I notice her gaze brushing over me. I'm used to relatives and friends of my patients assessing me. However, Margaret's gaze is kind. If I didn't know any better I'd even say it's bordering on sympathetic.

I place the mug in front of her and sit in a chair opposite her.

"Trent was very taken in with your accomplishments. He said you were one of the best," Margaret resumes the conversation.

I grimace. "Unfortunately, we're not making much progress in this particular instance."

She nods knowingly and takes a sip of her tea. "Cash can be quite stubborn."

"Trent warned me. I just had no idea. It's

impossible to get through to him." I hesitate, unsure how much to reveal. Truth be told, I'm so frustrated I feel like pouring a whole bucket of ice cold water over Cash Boyd's head to give him a wakeup call. I need to tell someone before I lose my self control and make an unprofessional move. "He needs to begin his therapy as soon as possible. We were supposed to start today, but as you can see, Mr. Boyd is not here. I've been spending hour after hour waiting for him to turn up. I don't even know where he is."

"Oh, dear." She shakes her head. "Hiding from you sounds like something he might do."

I cock my head, trying to make sense of her choice of words. "Is he shy?"

"Shy?" She lets out a laugh. "Goodness, no. Shy isn't a word I would ever use to describe Cash. He has his own mind, that one."

"Is he introverted?" A recluse, I want to add but abstain from it because the word might just carry a negative connotation for some.

She shakes her head again. "Far from it. Ever since the accident, he's been trying his best to make everyone's life harder, including his. I'm surprised you haven't left yet."

I frown. "Harder? How so?"

She leans forward and her voice drops to a conspiratorial whisper. "I shouldn't say this, but...the last therapists didn't fare too well. The longest they stayed was two days."

"They probably took his check and left," I say dryly.

"A check?" Her brows rise.

"He offered me twice what Trent's paying me to leave."

"Of course. It had to be money. That's how he got

rid of them so quickly." She frowns but there's also a glint of pride in her eyes. "His father and I always wondered how he did it. We decided that he might have scared them away. Apparently, money can buy everything." She lets out a laugh, and her eyes fix on me again. "But you stayed."

I shrug. "I want to help him. That's all. His offer wasn't more appealing than that."

"Not even double your paycheck?"

I shrug again. How can I tell her that I could have made good use of that money, but in the end my professional reputation is worth so much more than that?

"Not even that. But we can't work together if he's never around," I mutter. "Do you have any idea where I might find him?"

So I can pour that bucket of water over his head.

"God knows. He could be anywhere." She smiles kindly. "The best thing you can do is ignore him. He'll get bored quickly."

"How do you know?"

"He does it all the time, dear. To all of us," Margaret says. "Now, between you and me? I reckon he's had a secret bunker built."

I smile because in all honesty, she must be joking. "I can't just wait for him to get bored from his own disappearing acts. He even tells me to leave. I need to do something."

I shouldn't be gossiping about my clients, but it feels good to talk. Even if Margaret can't really help me with my dilemma, she does know him better than I do, which in turn might help me find a way to get him to open up to me.

"You're doing more than you think. You help him by just being here." She places her hand on mine. "He knows you're here. He knows you care. If he really wanted you gone, he'd be doing worse things than telling you to leave to get you off his property."

"Like what?"

"Locking the door and barring the windows." Her mouth twitches. "He did it a few times. Once, he didn't let me in for a week. He must have taken a liking to you."

"I don't think that's the case." The idea makes me blush, for some reason. He does like me, but not in the way she thinks.

"Just be patient. Cash always had a mind of his own. His passion for bull riding is just one example."

"Why does he do it knowing that he's risking his life?" I know the question is superfluous the moment I ask it. It's like asking why people race cars or jump out of planes.

He likes to take risks. It's as simple as that. But just because I see it all the time doesn't mean I understand the idea behind it.

"He's obsessed with it," Margaret says. "Taming bulls has always fascinated him, but at some point it became his sport. Trent used to take him to watch, and one day—and I remember the day well—Cash declared that he wanted to try it."

"You must have been with the Boyds for a long time."

The expression in her eyes grows warm. "A very long time. After Cash's mother died, I helped Trent with the house. Raising four kids on your own isn't easy, so we all pitched in, cooking meals, helping with the cleaning. The Boyd kids became like my own. When Clara died, I cried for their loss until I had no tears left. As if losing their mother wasn't enough of a tragedy. They also had to lose their sister."

I don't want to pry and yet I find myself asking,

"Their sister?"

"Yeah. Clara was military. The eldest of the kids, and so responsible. Grown up for her age." Her eyes focus on me as she ponders whether to disclose more. "She died in a bomb blast."

"I'm sorry," I whisper, even though I know no words can express the kind of sympathy any loss deserves.

"So am I." She sighs and a tear rolls down her cheek. She wipes it away quickly and shakes her head. "The best thing about getting older is that you get wiser. You learn how to let go. You learn to appreciate what you have and let go of the things that don't matter. The hate. The worries. The stress. Even beauty. You learn that even beauty is fleeting. That you don't need it to be happy. All that matters in life is family." She glances away and her gaze grows distant as though she's a million miles away again. "Cash has always been stubborn. You can't win a fight with him, so don't even try. After his sister's death, that trait of his just got worse. It made him fearless. A rebel. He threw all caution to the wind and just went for whatever he set his mind to. We all warned him not to ride that beast of a bull, but he wouldn't listen. To this day, he's adamant that he only fell because he lost his focus."

Taking in her words, I begin to form a picture of the kind of man Cash is. Stubborn and fearless, but maybe also a little bit hurt and as a result afraid of losing control. Maybe I can work with that. Maybe that's the side to reach out to.

We finish drinking our tea, and then Margaret gets up, her face strained as she places a hand on her lower back. "My age is working against me. I think I've pulled a muscle."

"Can I help?" Without waiting for her response, I

round the dining table and gently shove her hand aside to examine her back. As I begin to massage her tensed muscles, she closes her eyes and relaxes into my touch.

"Only if you let me show you around. There are plenty of things to do when Cash isn't around. Do you like gardening?"

"Gardening?" I smile at the idea of me growing and eating anything that hasn't come out of a grocery bag. "I'm far from having a green thumb."

"I'm sure you do. You just haven't discovered it yet." She turns to me and motions for me to follow her. "Let me show you the greenhouse. It's very relaxing. You're going to love it."

**

It's late afternoon when I return, my hands, and arms dirty from helping Margaret, my hair smelling of sun, flowers, and nature.

The sun's still high in the clear sky, burning everything with its harsh, unrelenting rays, but there's also a shift in the air. I can almost feel the oncoming rain and can hear the splattering sound against the windowpanes. It will make such a nice change from the relentless heat and the deadly silence of the house.

The house is as quiet as I left it, and there's still no sign of Cash. My stomach rumbles, reminding me that I haven't eaten, but I'll tackle that issue after a shower.

Stepping into the bathroom, I close the door behind me and proceed to undress. I look like a mess. Dirt cakes my face. Brown stripes of sweat and dust from carrying heavy bags of soil streak my skin. I probably smell as bad as I look. But my hands and nails are the worst.

I jump into the shower to wash off the dirt, but as I turn on the faucet, I realize there's no water. Frowning, I walk the small distance to the basin and try both the hot and cold water.

Nothing.

"What the hell?" I grab a fluffy white towel, ignoring the fact that it's going to be a dark shade of gray soon. Wrapping the towel around my body, I walk back to the kitchen where the sink is.

Again, no water.

There are only two possible explanations. Either Cash has a plumbing problem or—

My blood begins to boil in my veins.

"Cash!" I yell. No reply. I head for his bedroom and bang on his door. "Cash! Open up." I'm so angry I'm completely oblivious to the fact that I'm only wearing a towel that barely covers my modesty. "I know there's nothing wrong with your plumbing, so switch on the damn water."

I bang harder and then press my ear against the door to listen for any movement. When nothing stirs, I open the door and peer inside his bedroom.

He's not here.

I let out a frustrated groan.

How am I supposed to clean up without any water? Sweat is clinging to every inch of my body, and I can feel an itch spreading all over me. I'm about to close the door when I spy the open door to his bathroom.

A bathroom that comes with a shower and what looks like a generously sized bathtub.

This is heaven.

"I shouldn't," I mumble, closing my eyes. It would be completely unprofessional. Then again, I wouldn't be in this situation if he hadn't turned off the water. "Crap."

Before I can change my mind, I cross his bedroom in a few long strides.

The bathroom is bigger than mine with marble tiles and a huge bathtub. There's even a monstrous walk-in shower that can accommodate at least two.

It all feels so wrong.

Guilt starts tugging at me because of the fact that I'm invading his privacy.

What if I'm wrong and Cash didn't switch off the water. Maybe he has a plumbing problem and there's a leakage somewhere.

I can't blame him without concrete proof.

As I turn on the faucet, water starts pouring into the tub—warm and oh-so-inviting. It's much warmer than mine, which, come to think of it, always borders on icy.

"Son of a bitch," I whisper.

This is all the proof I need. Cash is doing this on purpose, maybe to get rid of me. My mind's made up. I'm not leaving. If he's trying to make my job harder than it already is, then I'm going to make him work harder than he's worked in his entire life.

I'll help him while turning into his worst nightmare. I'm going to be relentless...starting today.

As soon as I've cleaned up, I'm going to comb through every single spot in his house to find him.

But first...

Sighing with delight, I close the door to his bathroom and drop the towel to the floor.

Unprofessional or not, I sure as hell won't be running around dirty while he's laughing his ass off. First, I'll use his bathroom, and then I'll turn the tables.

I'll be exactly what he doesn't expect me to be. He

won't even see it coming.

CHAPTER SEVEN

CASH

THE SHOWER'S RUNNING. I can hear it through the closed door that's standing between us.

Oh, wait. It's not the shower. The flow is heavier and steadier, like a mad rush.

Erin's taking a bath...in my bathroom.

The knowledge excites me, arouses me.

It's pure deliciousness.

Letting out a low groan, I imagine her naked legs propped up against the wall of the tub. Her soft skin covered in thousands of bubbles. Her head thrown back. Maybe a hand between her legs, stroking herself.

Damn!

The thought of her fingers inside her tight little pussy is both hot and undeniably painful.

I'm pulsating with want. My balls are heavy and bursting, begging for release. I'm undoubtedly attracted to her. Wanting her when I should hate her. Getting all worked up just because a damn woman is using my bathroom, possibly masturbating.

Maybe she's imagining me while she's doing it.

The odds are definitely in my favor. I've met my fair share of women and recognize the signs of someone being attracted to me.

Holding my breath, I fight the urge to storm right in there and get a reaction from her. Maybe even force her to acknowledge our attraction.

My cock twitches, reminding me that both Miss Prissy and I would benefit from a little action between the sheets right now.

The faucet is turned off.

I'm waiting for a moan, a scream, maybe even something vibrating. I'm begging for an image, for a clue—anything that would keep my mind busy for the next few nights.

"Cash." Erin's voice carries over. "Don't even pretend you're not standing in front of the door like a creep because I *know* you're out there."

I bang my head against the door, heaving a dramatic sigh. "What gave me away?"

There is a small pause. I can hear her shifting in the water, splashing it around. "Your shadow. You realize how creepy you are, right?"

My lips twitch. "Creepier than the fact you're using my bathroom without asking?"

"Admit it. You didn't give me a choice. Do you have any idea how frustrating it is to arrive home dirty, and you can't even wash your hands?"

More frustrating than having blue balls? I want to ask. Or that I'm dying here trying to imagine her naked?

My hands grab the door handle, readying myself in case she gives me the go-ahead sign. "Let me come in, Erin."

There's a short pause before she replies, "Absolutely not."

"Fine." I lean against the door, my shoulder resting against the wood. "In that case, we need to talk."

"About what?"

"I don't know how to make it clear to you that I

want you to quit your job."

She lets out a groan that unfortunately doesn't resemble the moan I've been waiting for—not even in my wildest fantasies. The water sloshes around the tub. A few seconds later, the door opens. It's only a slit but I can make out that her hair's wet and one of my towels is wrapped around her glorious body.

For an instant, all I can think about is that I want to be that towel.

With the light streaming in through the high bay window and her face free of makeup, she looks younger, more carefree. The scent of my shower gel wafts over.

I imagine myself rubbing the shower gel onto her skin. Massaging her to get more lather. Pressing her dripping wet body against mine.

The thought's driving me crazy with want.

"Why?" Erin asks, interrupting my little fantasy with her.

The question's simple enough, yet I've no idea what the hell's she talking about. "Why, what?"

"Why do you want me to leave?"

"Because we can't work together," I clarify, leaving out the part that I could never focus on any kind of work with someone like her around. She's too sexy, too much of a distraction.

"You don't want my help. I get it," she starts. "You think accepting anyone's help would make you appear weak. But you need the training. You need to get your muscles working the right way. You need someone who'll push you to go beyond your limits."

"I can do that on my own, thank you," I mumble.

Her eyes meet mine through the open slit. "Please, be honest with yourself. You can't. It doesn't work that way. You need the physical therapy to help your joints regain mobility. If you don't start soon, your muscles will get weaker. They'll become incapable of supporting the injured structures, which, and I'm sure I don't have to tell you, will predispose you to further injury. Trust me, you don't want that...unless you don't mind being in pain and on painkillers for the rest of your life. No patient can ever do it on their own."

"I'm not taking any pain killers."

She sucks in a sharp breath. "Right. That's very brave of you, but it doesn't change a damn thing." Her gaze holds mine. "I'm only here to help, Cash. Don't make it hard on us."

"It's Cash, now? What happened to Mr. Body?" I cast her a sideways grin, which she doesn't return. She swings the door open and peers out, exhaling a heavy sigh. She's growing frustrated, I can tell by the frown on her face and the annoyed look in her eyes. But I can't help myself.

She is too naked, too close, too sexy. From up close, with half her breasts on full display and my towel barely covering her ass, she looks more perfect than in the daydreams I've been having about her. My lusting for her is slowly turning into a ravaging hunger. I take her in, all of her, while fighting the urge to rip off her clothes and take her right here, on this very spot, on the floor, against the wall, in as many ways as I can get her.

I want to bind her to my bedpost and fuck her day and night. I can almost taste her skin, smell her scent as she comes with my name on her lips. "You know what would make me feel better?"

"What?" she asks warily.

"Kissing you." My gaze trails her lips. They're full and ripe, and so very ready for me. "I want to kiss you, Erin."

Her breath hitches, and her eyes grow just a little bit wider. But it's not with shock.

It's arousal.

For a few seconds, she's rendered speechless, her emotions clearly written across her face.

She wants it. She wants me.

"You can't kiss me," she protests weakly.

"Why not? It's not like you don't want me to." I inch toward her, closing some of the inches between us, as I watch her reaction. "Right?"

Her eyes shimmer with want, her silence affirming my words.

She doesn't need to declare her attraction to me. It's right there, reflected in the way her chest is heaving and her lips seem to part just for me. Her gaze lingers on my mouth, then lifts back up to my eyes, as if she's indeed considering it. Imagining it. Weighing the ups and downs.

The knowledge turns me on.

My heart slams against my chest. My breathing grows heavy, labored.

"You want it as much as I want you. Don't pretend otherwise, Erin." I close the last bit of distance between us, bringing my mouth so close to hers, our breaths intermingle. "I can't imagine two people living together and be attracted to one another, not pursuing that attraction. It's not possible. Not with a woman like you."

Her brows shoot up. "A woman like me?"

"Yes. Someone who's going to have to touch me on a daily basis. I'm a man. I can't have your fingers all over me and not think of sex. So, let's skip the part where I'm lusting after you like a teen, and do something about it."

I know the moment she touches me, I'll go wild for her. How could I not? She's beautiful, sexy, and she lives with me.

"Let me get this straight." She bites her lip, thinking. "Your solution is to act on it? Do you think it will go away and then you'll be able to focus on therapy?" She sounds doubtful.

"It would definitely help."

She hesitates. "Just a kiss, Cash. Nothing more."

"Okay. One kiss." I can barely contain a smile. She's about to agree.

"A real kiss?" Erin asks.

"As real as it can get." I lean into her and brush my lips against her earlobe. "You would be helping me. Very much so. What do you say?"

She remains silent. She needs a final push.

"You want to, Erin," I whisper. "Want to know how I know?" My finger strokes her collarbone, tracing it gently. "A pulse never lies. Your heart's beating so fast, I can almost hear it."

"Maybe I want to, Cash," she says slowly. "But make no mistake. After this one time, it's back to business. I want to be able to do my job. I'm not giving up on you." She sounds hesitant, guarded; her words are slow and measured, as if speaking them out loud could turn out to be a mistake.

There's one thing that will give her the final push.

I know what she wants to hear. And I'm going to give it to her, even if it's not the truth.

"One kiss will dispel this attraction. It often does. Getting that part out of the way will help with the therapy or whatever you have in mind."

My hand moves past her collarbone to the nape of her neck as I bring my lips close to her mouth. She smells of shower gel and something else—a scent that's been lingering around the house since the day she arrived.

It reminds me of vanilla and sugar, of the kind of candy I want to lick and suck into my mouth. I don't know if it's her perfume, her skin, or just her, but it's delicious.

I imagine myself licking her skin, biting into her shoulder, and leaving my mark on her. My hand fists in her silky soft hair, and my mouth crushes against hers.

Her lips part instantly, willing, and her tongue tangles with mine. Her lips feel hot. But her tongue...it's the temperature of lava.

Damn.

It's a hell of a good kiss.

It's the highlight of my day.

No, make it the highlight of my year.

My whole being hums with excitement. My pants bulge from the tension and the want surging through me, and my body is on fire as our tongues tango in the kind of erotic dance that tells me this attraction is anything but easily dispelled.

I don't know how Dad stumbled across her, but I thank the stars for bringing her to me. I let my tongue dip in and out of her hot mouth. We touch and lick until it feels as though my heart might just burst out of my chest, and the crotch of my pants will rip at the seams.

With each kiss, I feel free. With each stroke of our tongues, I feel alive. With every shudder, she becomes a part of my soul.

We are attuned to each other, our tongues splitting time with our souls. With every breath, I can feel something resonating.

Crashing. Rising. Melting.

A kiss is never going to be enough. Maybe I can fool her, but I can't fool myself. The sexual attraction between us is too strong, too relentless. It's affecting my work, my exercising regime, my sleep. All I can do is think about her, and it's driving me insane.

My hands settle around Erin's wrists, and I lift them above her head. She gives a little moan of approval as the towel drops to the floor. My mouth remains glued to hers, but I can feel her nakedness against me.

I want her. Badly. If I don't take what I want, and soon, I'll be sporting a hard-on for the rest of her stay.

She's shaking beneath my strong grip. Deep down I know she wants me just as badly as I want her. Using my bad knee, I nudge her legs open. She presses her hips against me, as I wedge myself between her thighs, my mouth conquering hers again and again. My hand moves between her legs, stroking that delicious little spot that's as sweet as heaven, and damn, she's wet for me.

I stroke her gently, rubbing my fingers against her sweet spot, and we kiss until our breaths come short and ragged.

We kiss until she grinds her hips into me, until I know I could bring her to the edge.

"Do you feel how much I want you?" I whisper and press my erection into her. My words make her freeze.

Shit.

She pries her mouth away from mine and struggles out of my grip.

Her cheeks are ablaze, and her eyes shimmer

with awareness, as if my words have made her realize the impact of our intimate encounter.

I should have kept my stupid mouth shut.

"God, Cash." She takes a deep breath, half panting, half moaning. "This is going to stop right now." Leaving the towel at her feet, as she dashes back into the bathroom and slams the door behind her.

I stare at the closed door. "You can't be serious."

It takes her a full minute to answer. "I'm sorry, Cash. I can't do this. Trust me when I say, stopping now is for the best."

"Are you sure? Because it doesn't sound like you are." I'm so sexually frustrated I could slam my fist into the wall.

She sighs. "I'm very sure. I'm sorry. Please, let's just stay away from each other for a while."

"It was a just a kiss."

"No." I can imagine her shaking her head as she draws out the word. "No, it was way more than that. It was a mistake. Us having sex isn't going to help you. I should never have gone this far. Please, accept my apology. It was unprofessional of me. I don't know what I was thinking."

"You weren't thinking. You were feeling. We both need—" I struggle to find the right word. "Relief."

"I should have known better. You're my patient. I'm sorry."

"If you keep saying sorry one more time I swear I'll—" I rake my fingers through my hair, unsure what the hell I'll be doing. The thing is she's blowing hot and cold. I want her, but I can't have her, even though she wants it, too.

Her bullshit about professionalism is infuriating.

"You know what? You're right," I say. "It's unprofessional of you to make me want you the way I do, and then leave me in physical pain."

"That wasn't my intention at all. Tomorrow we'll try a different approach. Something that will take your mind off of things."

I laugh. She can't be serious.

Nothing could ever take my mind off the hot little pussy I can probably smell on my fingers.

But then she adds, "I promise we'll start slow. You'll see therapy will make you feel so much better. You'll be back to your old self in no time."

That instantly kills the mood.

My old self.

She just won't let me forget it.

I grab the towel off the floor and knock on the door to make sure I have her attention. "Now's a good time to quit."

"What?"

"Quit," I say, this time louder. "Time for you to leave."

"You can't be serious." She sounds incredulous, but I can already hear the angry undertones in her voice. "You tell me to leave after we've just made out? You're a prick, Mr. Boyd."

"We're back to Mr. Boyd, huh? Make up your mind, woman."

"The answer's 'no.' I'm not quitting. I told you before, and I'll say it again," Erin yells.

"You will...once you realize you're wasting your time."

A small bang resonates from the walls. Did she just slam her hand against the door? Or maybe it was her head. I grin, imagining her beautiful eyes shimmering with anger and her breasts heaving with every furious breath she takes.

Oh, how much I would pay just to see her naked and shaking with rage.

"You made me kiss you," she hisses.

"Because you wanted it as much as I did," I say coolly.

"No, I didn't. I only agreed because you claimed you'd let me do my job. You said it would help with your therapy."

"Your words, not mine, sweetheart."

She groans in exasperation. "Those were *exactly* your words."

She must be fuming by now. I bet her skin's all flushed and hot, and so very ready for my touch.

"You tricked me. Go away, Mr. Boyd."

"I'm afraid I can't, sweetheart. This is my house. If someone has to leave, then that's definitely you."

That shuts her up for a few seconds. I can almost hear her mind working, considering my words.

"Fine," she calls out eventually.

I strain to make sense of the shuffling sounds behind the door. After what feels like an eternity, the door swings open and Erin dashes past me, making sure not to get too close.

"You're leaving?" I ask. "Like, really leaving?"

She comes to a halt near the door, which is as far away from me as my room allows. "Did I mention you're a prick?"

"You did." I wink. "Can't say I agree with you, but I'm happy to play along."

"I'm not leaving," she says, jutting out her chin. "Not until I've found you the help which I'm not even sure you deserve. And your kisses suck. You're the worst kisser in the whole world."

"I would believe you if you weren't so wet." My

lips curl upward at the shade of red covering her cheeks. "You thought I wouldn't notice? Your pussy never lies. In fact, I can still smell you on my fingers."

To prove my point, I lift my fingers and take a whiff, then proceed to run my tongue over my fingertips. "You even taste like you're hot for me."

She turns a brighter shade of red, if that's even possible.

"Prick." With that, she slams the door behind her.

Laughing, I drop onto my bed.

CHAPTER EIGHT

ERIN

MAKING OUT WITH Cash Boyd was never part of the plan. I don't know why I let him persuade me into doing it. In fact, I'm pretty sure he tricked me.

Groaning, I sink onto my bed and press a pillow against my face.

Let's be honest.

No one forced me into doing it. It was my own free will. I even enjoyed myself way more than I should have, which is why I was wet.

Very wet.

I can't believe the prick noticed it. I can't believe he even licked my juices off his fingers. The mere thought of Cash's tongue between my legs leaves me breathless with anticipation and want.

We were so close to doing way more than a little bit of tongue acrobatics. It took every ounce of my willpower to tear myself away from his hard body. The only thing that kept me from going all the way was the image of Cash's father.

What would Trent think if I fucked his son?

How would I feel if I broke my own rules and engaged in bedsheet activities with my client?

Granted, he's only half my client, given that he's not paying me. But still.

Even if he's not the one paying me, would it be enough to revoke my license as a therapist? Maybe not, but our patient-to-therapist relationship would be tarnished, and I would have to move back to Chicago. Return to my tiny apartment. To the rush and the excitement that comes with city life.

There would be another job. Another patient while Cash would disappear from my life.

My throat chokes up.

He'll disappear anyway, which is exactly what I want.

Right?

The sooner, I'm gone, the better. While I might have enjoyed his touch way more than I should have, his motivations are clouded by his injury. He's like every other patient in his age group who's spending a little too much time with his female therapist.

Which is why I can't let the lines blur, why I can't let my own desire meddle with my job.

Cash is easily the hottest guy I've ever met, but he's still my patient.

There is an attraction between us. No doubt about that. But I can see that this attraction's been a little too much on my mind lately, it might just complicate my job to the point of rendering me unable to fulfill my duties.

He's going to need more help than I can offer him if my mind's clouded and we can't keep a professional distance.

Prick or not, Cash's recovery needs to remain my priority. Besides, I won't let his father down.

Cash might think he has his life in working order, that just because he can partly walk, he'll get back to his old self on his own. But he doesn't realize that sooner or later, without therapy, his injuries will gain the upper hand.

His muscles will weaken, making him prone to more injury. Eventually, making a full recovery will become impossible.

I won't let that happen.

Having made up my mind, I type a quick text message on my cell phone, ready to take the next step that's best for him.

***

The phone flashes with a photo of Ally's grimacing face almost instantly. I take the video call on the second ring.

"You want me to do *what*?" Ally's brown hair is in disarray, her gaze harried as usual, like she already has one foot headed out the door. We've been best friends for ages, even went to school together and walked down the same career path. But while I'm the one who's devoted her entire life to my job, she has never seen it as her passion, which is why I can rely on her not to be too tied down to jump in for me at the last minute.

"I want you to take the next flight to Montana and do this job," I say matter-of-factly.

Her eyes narrow. "Why? I thought you were excited about it. What changed?"

"Because—" I cringe inwardly. Ally's the one person I've never lied to, mostly because she's always had my back. She never judges, which is why I know I'm safe revealing the truth. But that doesn't make speaking it out loud any easier. "We made out."

"Who did?"

Peering at the closed door, I lower my voice. "I made out with my patient."

"You did what?" She doesn't just sound genuinely shocked; she also looks the part. Who could blame her? As a physical therapist that's the one thing you never, ever do. It's textbook knowledge.

"I know." I wince. "It's just that he's hot and I don't know what's gotten into me. I—" I break off because I know *exactly* what's gotten into me.

Six-foot-three of hard muscles, an accent that could whisper dirty things into my ear all night, and smoldering green eyes I want to peer into as I moan his name.

"I can't help you." Ally jerks me out of my reverie.

"You can't?" I ask, dumbfounded.

"I have this new job and—"

"Oh." I stare at her face, unsure whether I've just heard her right.

"In fact, I'm headed out the door this minute. But call me if I can help you with anything else."

She's trying to wriggle her way out of it. I just

know it from the way her gaze darts around, avoiding my eyes.

"Did I mention how much it pays?" I hurry to add before she hangs up on me.

Her expression doesn't change. That's when it dawns on me. Ally's a city girl through and through. Relocating to Montana, if only for a short period of time, is probably the equivalent of relocating to Northern Alaska to her.

She shakes her head. "No. But like I said I—"

"You're lying." She is. I know it. "There's no important job, is there, Ally? You just don't want to fly down here."

She looks so guilty, it's almost comical.

"Sorry," she mumbles. "But I'm sure you'll do just fine. Just don't get involved with the guy. Got to go. Love you."

With that, she hangs up.

I stare at the black screen for a minute or two, unable to comprehend what just happened.

"Unbelievable," I mutter, wondering who else I could call.

Ally was my best bet. I know a few fellow physical therapists, but I don't trust any of them. If someone finds out that I made out with my patient, my license could be gone forever.

I can't trust Cash not to spill the beans, either. He might do it out of spite, maybe not with the intention to hurt my career chances, but simply because he might not understand the implications of the situation.

"Un*fucking*believable," I repeat.

Looks like I'm stuck with Cash Boyd, whether I want to be here or not.

What the hell was I thinking?

CHAPTER NINE

ERIN

AFTER MY CONVERSATION with Ally, I decide to spend the rest of the day in my room, not least because I can't trust my judgment around Cash Boyd.

A part of me can't stop wondering what would have happened if I allowed more than just a kiss.

Would we have been able to stop?

Would he still have wanted me to leave?

No one's ever asked me whether he could kiss me. Not the way Cash did, anyway, with forceful determination and the kind of desire that only managed to ignite my own flame of want. And certainly never a guy like him, who can make me feel discombobulated with a single glance.

I've also never enjoyed kissing a man as much as I've enjoyed kissing him, losing myself in the moment, forgetting the where and when. My mouth is still tingling whenever I press my fingers against my lips, as though he's somehow seared himself into me, branding my body, preparing me for more to come.

I go to bed thinking of him, consumed by the memory of his knowing lips against mine, contrasted by the rough sensation of his stubble grazing my cheeks. I search for the quiet only sleep can provide, but his presence infiltrates even my dreams, haunting me, taunting me, punishing me for being so weak.

Even in my dreams, I want him. And after our kiss, I seem to want him even more.

The theoretical part of my brain tells me that I should have pushed him away. However, the chemical part of me, the one that gets all of my juices flowing, asks me to do the opposite. It's the latter part that I fear most because it renders me unpredictable.

I spend the following morning gardening while chatting with Margaret, who's just as eager for the company as I am, albeit for different reasons.

She isn't just slowly turning into a nice diversion from my consuming thoughts about Cash, she's also becoming a friend. Maybe because she reminds me of my dear, sweet Grandma with her good nature and non-inquisitive nature.

It's early evening when I return from the greenhouse, my body tensing at hearing the angry voices echoing through the hall.

"I made myself clear that I don't need help. I can manage on my own." Cash's voice booms from the kitchen, followed by clattering pots and cutlery.

Holding my breath, I tiptoe down the hall, unsure whether to turn around and give him privacy or storm in to make sure he's all right.

"I've traveled all the way from Florida to see you. You don't get to tell me whether I can help you or not, Cash Boyd." The woman's voice sounds just as angry and forceful. I flinch at the impact she has on me, even though I'm not even the target of her wrath.

She doesn't sound like Margaret. Is it his girlfriend? Wife? I haven't seen a ring on his finger, but that doesn't mean a thing.

My heart gives a sharp pang at the thought of them fighting because of our kiss.

God.

I'm such a slut.

"Fine. Suit yourself, Shannon. But I'm telling you—"

"Don't you dare! I promised on your mother's grave I'd make sure you boys don't get into shit. And what you're doing is beyond shit. It might even be the shittiest stunt you've pulled so far."

"Leave my mother out of this," Cash yells. "She would have known to—"

I flinch at the sound of a slap. I really hope they're not hitting each other. The woman laughs, cutting him off. "She would have known to slap some wits into you for being an arrogant idiot, Cash. Getting on that bull was idiotic enough. But being a jerk about it and getting on everyone's nerves by insisting that you don't need help"—she pauses, emphasizing the last few words—"is the icing on the cake. Now get out of my way, or I'll do as Lizzy would have done if she were still here. She might have let you use such a tone with her, but you're not doing it with me. My sister's probably thanking me from Heaven right now for teaching you some manners."

Is she his aunt? I stare at the door, wondering.

Something clatters to the floor, the sound reverberating off the walls. Startled, I take a step back. An instant later, Cash storms out—well, more like stumbles out, his beautiful face a mask of annoyance and pain.

He barely acknowledges me as he hurries past with unsteady steps, his leg in a weird angle, mumbling something that sounds like, "Get that woman the hell out of my house."

I stare after him as he turns the corner, wondering what's going on. Should I get mixed up in this? Whomever he's been fighting with, it's none of my business, and yet it is because he's my patient and I'm supposed to keep him focused on regaining the full mobility of his leg.

Which hasn't been an easy task so far.

I don't know how he did it, but Cash managed to avoid me for all of three days. I've been combing each and every room at least six times a day. He needs to begin his therapy. However, he's never around, even though I could swear I've heard noises a few times.

I can only suspect he has a hidden spot somewhere I'm not aware of, just as Margaret told me.

I've no idea when and if he prepared himself anything to eat the last few days, but I sure as hell didn't do it for him.

All I've been doing so far is setting up my gear in the morning, wait, and then wait some more. Then pack up again. Bang on his door. Call his name. Go for a walk to blow off some steam. Take a cold shower, because the hot water's not working.

Rinse and repeat.

This drama has to end.

"Hi!" I peer through the open kitchen door at the blonde woman rummaging through the kitchen counters with the fury and speed of someone on a serious mission.

She looks younger than Margaret.

"Oh, hi. You must be Erin." She slams the refrigerator door and turns to face me, the thin skin around her eyes wrinkling into countless fine lines as she shoots me a generous smile. In spite of the fact that she must be at least two decades older than me, she has a youthful flair about her. Wearing a black pencil skirt with a tight top and black stilettos, and with her hair curled, she looks like she's about to head out to some office party. The tight top pushing her breasts almost up to her chin is most definitely helping with the youthful look.

I like her instantly, not least because she's the only friendly face I've seen since Cash's father and Margaret.

"I'm Shannon." She pushes a hand with bright pink nail polish my way. As I'm reaching out to shake it, she grabs me in a quick but tight hug, which almost knocks the air out of my lungs.

Why can't Cash be so friendly?

Then again, I'm not sure how I'd feel having his hard body pressed against mine again. The first time was enough to cause me a few hot dreams. And oh, that kiss...I wouldn't mind repeating that experience.

"I'm Shannon," she says and releases me. "Cash's aunt."

"I can come back another time," I offer. "I wouldn't want to be a nuisance."

"No, silly. Stay!" She shakes her head and purses her lips. "You're not a nuisance. That would be Cash. That boy will be the death of us all." She shakes her head again.

I don't want to point out that "that boy" is an adult male in his late twenties and from the looks of his house, very much in control of his life.

Unlike me.

Then again, that's exactly why I'm here.

"I was looking for you anyway," she says. "Trent told me you arrived a week ago. I would have come sooner, but work has been busy. Life is busy. And Cash, he is a handful. I thought I'd give you some time to adjust to your new life because Cash isn't exactly—"

She waves her hand in the air, leaving the rest unspoken, but despite the irritation reflected in the expression on her face, there's a warmth to the way she says his name. "Let's just say, he should be glad he isn't *my* son." She laughs, and her eyes flicker with warmth.

It's obvious she cares about him a lot.

"I haven't seen him around much," I offer, unsure how to react to her statement.

"Doesn't surprise me. That one's always been up to something."

Her response sparks my curiosity. "You're his aunt, you say?"

She nods. "His mother and I were sisters. I would like to go over a few things with you if that's okay?"

I nod my agreement and she motions for me to sit down at the mahogany dining table. She pours two cups of coffee, and then perches on the chair opposite from mine, pushing a cup toward me.

I take a sip of the frothy concoction and can't help

but guzzle down half the cup after days of no coffee because I couldn't find the coffee maker. He's most certainly hidden it to spite me.

"Where are you from?" Shannon resumes the conversation.

"Port Huron, Michigan. But I've spent most of my life in Chicago." I force myself to set the cup down to look at her.

"Is that where your heart is, Erin?"

"That's a strange question." I laugh even though the question makes me uncomfortable.

"Maybe." Her gaze sweeps around the kitchen. "You said Cash has been giving you trouble? What's he been up to this time?"

"Sorry?" The sudden change in subject takes me off guard. It takes a few moments for her words to register. "He hasn't been trouble. He's managed to avoid me for days. Margaret thinks he has a secret bunker, but I believe there's a hidden passageway or something inside his house, or how else could he possibly manage to sneak past me every day?" I laugh at the ridiculousness of my idea.

Her gaze pierces into me, assessing me. "What makes you think that?"

"Well,"—I hesitate—"for starters, I've been hearing noises, but then, when I head out—"

"He isn't anywhere to be found." Her lips purse. For a moment, her eyes shimmer with something, and I'm sure she's about to divulge a secret. But the impression disappears quickly. "You know, my ex-husband, Trent's brother, owned a construction company. That was before I moved to Florida. Anyway, he did all the refurbishing for Cash a few years ago. I could get you the blueprints."

"I don't think that's necessary. I wasn't being serious."

"Still...I'll have Josh get you a copy." At my questioning look, she adds, "Josh is my son, so if you need anything and can't get a hold of any of us, my son's the one to call. Or Kellan, Cash's brother. He doesn't live far from here." Reaching into her purse, she pulls out a sheet of paper and pushes it across the table toward me. I peer at the neat scribbling—rows and rows of names, their connection to Cash and the corresponding phone numbers.

I stare agog. There's at least forty people on there, all friends and family.

"It's a close community. We all care about Cash," Shannon says softly. "I don't know if Trent showed you what happened to him, but for a good few minutes we all thought he was dead."

"What happened?" I find myself asking even

though I know I shouldn't be prying or gossiping, and particularly not when it involves a patient. But I'm curious and eager to find out more about Cash's life, not least because I'm not sure Trent revealed the entire magnitude of the bull riding accident. Relatives can be just as traumatized as the patients. I can imagine that he has yet to come to terms with what happened to his son.

Shannon draws a sharp breath and releases it slowly before she speaks. "Cash has been obsessed with bull riding ever since he was a child. It's a bit of a tradition around here. Something young people do for fun. The bulls are vetted and mellow. Nothing too dangerous, you understand."

She raises her eyebrows. I nod, interested, even though I've heard the story before, and she continues, "Anyway, a few years back, Cash decided to take it to a whole new level, go pro. He signed up for one competition after another. Some people are addicted to skydiving or other dangerous activities. Cash gets his adrenaline rush from bucking bulls, and he's always looking for the most temperamental bull he can get. I wish I could say this was his first accident, but it's just one in a very long string of incidents that could have cost him his life. He's convinced that he can and will conquer every bull."

Frustration seeps from her voice.

"Obviously, I don't know him, but he seems like someone who knows what he's doing," I say. While I understand her concern, it is his life, after all.

She grimaces. Her blue eyes are overshadowed by worry as her hand squeezes my arm. The motion is gentle, but I can feel the unspoken imploration and urgency in it. "Is that what he told you?"

I open my mouth to appease her but she doesn't give me a chance. "He doesn't know shit. The real reason I'm here is because I wanted to see you."

"You wanted to see *me*?"

"Yes." She nods her head gravely. "I'm not sure whether Trent told you that Cash had a head injury three years ago."

"No one mentioned that."

She begins to stir sugar into her coffee, absentminded, and then takes a sip, grimacing. "A bull stomped on his head, cracking his skull. He spent weeks in the hospital, the doctors warned him to stay away from bull riding. You think he would have listened." Grimacing again, she stirs more sugar into her coffee—this time with such fervor I fear the mug might shatter and spill its contents all over the dining table. "Of course, he wouldn't. He jumped right onto the next bull. And the one after that. And so forth." She stops stirring and raises her gaze to meet mine. "He didn't take the warning seriously. He doesn't believe that another head injury could kill him. You see, Cash is Cash. He doesn't care if his life's at stake. Or that we're all worried sick about him. That he only dislocated his hip and broke a few bones in the process was a blessing for us. I know what I'm saying sounds horrible, but it's the truth." Her eyes shimmer with guilt, seeking my sympathy, understanding, approval. "What happened to him is bad, but we're also relieved because we still hope this might open his eyes. Or so we did until—" Inhaling a sharp, shaky breath, she spreads her hands on the table, her posture going rigid.

"Until what?" I ask, sensing what she's about to say.

"He said he'd do it again, if he could only walk. And we believe him."

"I don't think he'd—"

"You don't know him the way we do," Shannon says. "He hasn't given up on this passion of his. He hasn't learned anything from his mistakes. My son told me that Cash already inquired about entering the next competition. Which, if you ask me, is insane. He is insane." Tears form in her eyes, and her voice is shaking. "He takes one step, then another, and that's when things begin to escalate. That's what they always do. They escalate until there's no going back. Until it's too late. Why can't he see that?" She leans back, her face drawn in pain and frustration, her hands shaking. "I don't know how to stop him. None of us knows. This recklessness, foolishness, stupidity of his needs to stop. He isn't even back on his feet, and he's already thinking about playing with his life again. Why doesn't he see the pain and worry he's causing us?" She leans forward, her eyes narrowing on me as she squeezes my hand, the sudden gesture startling me. "I'm here because I need you to understand the magnitude of this. I need you to make sure he stays out of trouble. Don't encourage his passion. Don't tell him you admire it. Because the next time Cash is back on a bull, breaking a few bones won't be the only bad thing happening."

Her words chill me to the core—or maybe it's the grain of truth I sense in them that make me doubt the sanity of getting Cash back on his feet.

"I had no idea."

"This is what I wanted to ask of you. Please, make this clear to him. He hasn't been listening to his family. Maybe a stranger, a professional who's seen many injuries, will get the message across."

"I can try."

"Thank you," she says. "Trent said there's something about you, Erin. I think I agree. We all want him to walk again. But we also want him to return to the city, to that job of his, away from this brutal sport and the things that tempt him. If you could kill that passion of his, we'd all be grateful to you. God knows, all the Boyd boys have their vices, but none of them is ready to break their neck in the process. Not like Cash is."

Kill that passion.

She looks so hopeful; I find myself nodding my head, even though I don't even know how to get through to Cash, let alone talk him out of risking his life for fun.

Why the hell would he even listen to a stranger when his own family's wishes mean nothing to him?

"I'll try my best," I repeat.

"Thank you," she says. "I want to give you something." She retrieves her handbag and adds before I get a chance to decline, "It's just a little something to show you my gratitude."

I peer at her, uncomfortable, as she retrieves her purse. "No, please." She looks up, a frown perched on her forehead, as I continue, "I'm not doing this job for the money. I do it because I love it."

"You do?"

"Yes." I nod in the hope she won't persist. Trent's already paying me too much for doing nothing. I can't take her money, as well, and then end up crushing her high hopes.

It wouldn't be right.

She looks at me for a few seconds, then stashes the purse away. I can sense the change in subject before she speaks. "So, you are from Chicago?"

I nod.

"Is there someone special waiting for you back home?"

"I'm not seeing anyone," I say, unsure where she's headed with this.

"Your heart isn't back in Chicago then."

I laugh. "No, it certainly isn't."

She regards me intently for a few moments. "A man's heart plans his way, but the Lord directs his steps. Proverbs 16:9. You see, I believe everyone should be where their heart is, be it a place, a person, or even something they love doing."

"In that case, my heart's a nomad." I clear my throat to get rid of the sudden cotton sensation coating the cave of my mouth.

I thought my heart had found a home. Now I'm

sure that home was rather an old, dilapidated tool shed than my castle in the sky.

"You'll find it someday. Maybe even sooner than later."

"I'm not sure I want to," I mumble. "I haven't been excited about a place or a person in a very long time."

"Let me tell you something. I've been married three times. But I haven't given up hope on meeting that someone special one day, even though I'm not even sure the right one would put up with me." She laughs at my expression. "I can be quite overbearing. Bossy. Independent. Not many men are strong enough to deal with that."

"There's someone for everyone," I offer even though I don't believe that myself.

Shannon glances at her watch. "I would love to chat with you some more, but I've got to go," she says and jumps to her feet, back to her previous chirpy self. "The fridge is stocked up. I'll be back in a few days. If you need anything—"

"The list, I know." I follow her out into the hall.

She opens the door but stops in the doorway. "One more thing. The family's having a little get together this weekend. Nothing major." She waves her hand in the air. "We insist that you come. We all want to meet you."

I freeze on the spot, my hands suddenly cold and clammy. She's just being friendly; I'm aware of that, and yet I can't shake off the sudden tightening sensation squeezing my chest. While I don't mind meeting my patients' relatives, this does feel a little too personal.

"I don't think Cash should be moving around too much." My voice comes out a little too shaky.

"That's why we'll be hosting it in his backyard," Shannon says, oblivious to my reservations. "I'll call you with the details, but don't tell him. We need to rely on the surprise element of it. Otherwise, he might throw the door in our faces and lock himself inside for the next few weeks. That's what he did last time we tried to cheer him up." She winks at me.

I'm not sure whether she's joking or being serious, so I just nod my head.

Shannon grabs me in another tight hug, and then she's out the door, leaving me with a sense of unease in the pit of my stomach.

As I clean up the kitchen, her words keep ringing through my mind like an echo.

Prior to his accident, Cash suffered a head injury. And yet he continues to risk his life.

I want to help him, I really do. But what if I get

him back on his feet only for him to climb on the next bull?

Maybe next time he won't be so lucky and survive a fall.

CHAPTER TEN

CASH

I DON'T TRUST many people. I can count the number on one hand. My brothers, Kellan and Ryder, are two of them.

Doesn't mean I don't hate their guts right now.

Expecting my family to respect my privacy and need for solitude is too much to ask, which is probably why I moved away from Montana in the first place. Buried in my office, I only hear the turmoil of chatter and laughter when it's too late to slam the door in my visitors' faces.

I draw the curtains and head out through the secret door connecting the office with the walk-in closet in my bedroom. While my business ventures don't involve any criminal activities, some of the people I deal with aren't so transparent.

For that reason, I came up with the idea of hiding my private office from plain view and anyone who would want to rummage through my contacts, contracts, and receipts.

To the unaware, the door looks like an ordinary mirror. In the early remodelling stages of my home, the office was supposed to be turned into a panic room. Not that you'd ever need a panic room in Montana, but in my job, I deal with shady figures on a daily basis, so I figured it might not be such a bad idea.

Now, with my family grating on my nerves, and visitors coming unannounced all the time, the panic room has been turned into an office with a couch, refrigerator, and my very own microwave—just in case I need my privacy from the world for a while.

The real panic room is underground, and features nowhere in the remodelling plans.

Not that anyone but my close family and friends know where I live.

And now Erin.

I grimace. Just thinking her name causes a sudden stir inside my pants, which I attribute to my dick's lack of action and her being female. She is bestowed with a great pair of tits that she likes to hide behind the most unflattering work attire I've ever seen. And she has the most gorgeous lips I've ever kissed—soft and full.

She caught me off guard when she left my bathroom with only a towel wrapped around her. That kissing her would turn me on came as no surprise. What surprised me was the fact that, for a moment, she took the lead, as though she wanted more but didn't dare go for it.

I can be a total asshole when I'm sexually frustrated—and I've rarely been frustrated in my life. There's something about her that drives me mad and unable to think about anything but her, her body, her scent, her taste.

I want to blame it all on the accident and the subsequent lack of action between the sheets, but the truth is, I've lived a monk's life for the past few months. Abstaining was bearable.

Since Erin's arrival, abstinence has become no longer an option. She's someone I'd rather hear moaning my name in ecstasy than have her look at me with pity in her eyes. Combine that with the fact that I've never needed help from anybody, and particularly not from someone like her, and it's an explosive blend that's turned me into a walking rod of anger since her arrival.

The last few days, I made it my priority to avoid her while getting a good look at her whenever she ventured into the backyard. She seems to have developed a routine: search the veranda while calling my name a few times, then sit down on the stairs to type a few text messages, her whole body rigid with what I'm pretty sure is anger.

I don't know whether she's angry with me or the person she's communicating with. But either way, her anger doesn't distract from just how beautiful she looks in the bright sunlight, with her head bowed, unaware of the fact that she isn't alone.

I've been wondering whether she always kisses her patients, or whether I'm the exception to the rule. While the former wouldn't particularly please me, I want to repeat the experience.

"Cash. Get your sorry ass out here." My brother's voice reaches me a moment before he pounds against the door. If he keeps at it for another minute, I'll be sending him the bill for replacing the wood with steel.

"Kellan," I mutter and open the door, stifling the

need to punch him in the face. Yeah, that's what family does to you.

I head outside, making sure to close and lock the door behind me. Not that it's necessary. My brothers are the only ones who know of my panic room which is also my very own private space.

That's when I hear the chatter of voices and realize Kellan's brought the whole troop with him.

Needless to say, I'm not pleased.

"There you are. What the heck are you doing in there when you should be out here, celebrating?" Kellan points behind me with the leering grin of someone who wouldn't be surprised to find three chicks spread out naked on my bed.

"What exactly are we celebrating?"

He cocks his head. "Dude, don't you know what day it is today?"

"No. Why don't you enlighten me?"

His lips twitch. "Don't tell me you forgot your own birthday?"

My face falls.

Fuck!

Is that today?

"Happy birthday. You look older than you are." Kellan lets out an annoying laugh, then shouts to the commotion on the terrace, "Hey, folks. Cash is now also suffering from dementia."

"Keep the fuck quiet." I shuffle around the bend on my crutches, taking slow, mindful steps.

"Dude," Kellan continues, oblivious to my need for solitude. "I'm telling you. Hiding from the world all the time makes you mentally challenged."

"I very much doubt that," I mumble. "As for the hiding, I've had a very good reason."

He cocks his head to the side, regarding me intently. "I can't think of one, but please share it with me."

"I've been hiding because—" How can I spell out the obvious to my brother who seems to have forgotten all about the bachelor life he used to live before his soon-to-be wife, Ava, came along and put an end to it. There are certain rules involving the intricacies of dipping your dick into the dating pool without actually swimming in it. One being: don't ever let a woman invade your private space, unless you want her to take over.

"I've been avoiding Erin," I mutter.

"You've been avoiding your *physical therapist*?" Kellan repeats like I'm speaking Chinese.

"Yes." I nod slowly. "And I'd like to keep it that way."

His brows draw together. "Why?"

"Because Dad should never have sent her. I don't need anyone's help. I'm doing just fine on my own."

Kellan stares at me for a second, then bursts out in the kind of laughter that would grate on a saint's nerves.

"What?" I shrug my shoulders grimly. "What's so funny?"

He continues laughing. I glare at him until he's calmed down, but the flicker of amusement in his eyes doesn't blow out. "Don't tell me you haven't just broken your leg, but also your brain. If I weren't walking down the aisle soon—" He smacks his tongue, meaningfully. "Seriously, if I were you I'd seriously consider whether I might have lost more than just the mobility of my leg in that accident."

"What the hell are you talking about?"

"Your dick. I'm talking about your dick." He sighs and wraps an arm around my shoulders, drawing me closer. "Listen, bro. The way I see it, you should thank Dad for being an intrusive jerk. He's just tossed you a hot piece of ass right in front of your door, and you've been nothing but a sulky little kid about it. Don't tell me you haven't been thinking about tapping Erin because if you haven't, you don't need physical therapy. You need a shrink."

"I didn't ask Dad to hire someone as hot as her."

His hand moves to his ear, cupping it. "Did you just say hot?" His voice is dripping with amusement as he slams the palm of his hand against my back. "I'm glad to hear there's still hope for you. It took us six weeks to find the right person—basically a physical therapist with the right credentials, glowing recommendations from previous patients, and who'd be willing to live in the same house as the patient. It took us even longer than that to persuade her to travel to a town that's in the middle of nowhere. It sure helps that she's easy on the eye, funny, motivated—all things we didn't know before we first met her." He cocks a brow. "Want me to go on? I know you want to say it, so...." He shrugs. "You're welcome."

"She's not my type."

"Who cares whether she's your type? She's here to get you back on your feet." He laughs. "Besides, I don't believe you because you just called her hot. My advice? Let her spin her magic. It will be like a good ol' massage parlor, maybe even better."

His clueless remarks anger me for some reason. Erin isn't cheap. She's a professional. For some reason, I want him to respect that. "Do you have any idea what physical therapy is?"

"No, and I don't care either. That's for you to find

out. I'm not the one who was stupid enough to ride that bull. No offense."

"None taken."

While Kellan likes to dish out his advice and opinion to everyone, regardless of whether they might be interested in hearing it, I excel at doing the opposite of whatever people expect of me.

He obviously expects me to fuck her, which I might have...under different circumstances.

Kellan's brows shoot up meaningfully. "So, how long has it been exactly?"

Dammit!

He nudges me with his elbow, almost knocking off my balance. "I know you haven't had anyone over in ages."

I narrow my eyes. "How would you know that? Maybe I'm seeing someone you don't know about."

"You're not. Ryder's been watching the house." Catching my angry expression, Kellan shrugs. "What? We need to make sure you're okay. For all we know, you could slip on the hardwood floor, bang your head against the kitchen counter and lie there, choking on your own blood."

"That is a well planned-out scenario. Thank you for that. I bet you guys have been picturing it quite a few times," I say, dryly. "Why don't you add choking on an olive to your list of gory possibilities as to how I might meet my early demise?"

"Go on. Ridicule us all you want, but you've got to admit it is a very realistic scenario."

"Absolutely...if I were an old lady with a dislodged hip and in dire need of a walking stick." Breaking off, I shake my head. "Shit, Kellan. You always know how to make me feel better. You're an asshole."

The old lady bit is as unrealistic as it could get, but the dislodged hip part isn't that far from the truth.

Dad can be annoying under the best of circumstances, but he would never go as far as watching my house. Whenever I think my brothers couldn't get more in your face, trust Kellan and Ryder to come up with new ways to burst my bubble.

"That's what brothers are for," Kellan says. "You can pull that woe-is-me shit with Dad, but it's not working on us. We both know you enjoy the attention."

"As soon as I can walk, I'm going to punch you," I growl.

"Sounds good. Let me book you a date for next year. How does February sound?"

I know he tries to piss me off. It's my brother's

attempt to get me off my ass, make me work harder to get my old life back. While I appreciate the effort, I know it's fruitless. My old life's gone for good. But if I had been able to walk, I would have given him a black eye for all the comments he's been cracking the past few months.

"Book me in for this year." I give him the finger of my right hand, then the finger of my left hand. "I'll do it even if I have to chase you around on crutches."

I shuffle along the narrow path, freezing to the spot as I notice the commotion on my veranda.

"What the—"

Most of the Boyd clan's here. I spy Kellan's fiancée, Dad, Aunt Shannon, and a few of my cousins. No sight of my brother, Ryder. And at least no one invited the neighbors.

There's no way I'll be able to kick everyone's ass out. They'll just gang up on me, and I'll draw the shorter straw.

"I didn't realize there was going to be a public gathering in my house," I hiss at my brother, realizing too late why he's been grinning all this time. "I don't think I invited any of you over."

"Surprise." Kellan shoots me another one of his stupid grins. "You know you don't need to. It's your birthday, so naturally, we'll come anyway. That's what family's for."

Yeah, to annoy the hell out of me.

"You'll have to thank my fiancée for this awesome idea," he continues.

I peer at Ava, my soon-to-be sister-in-law, and my bad mood lifts a little. She's sitting on a lounger, her pregnant belly so huge I'm pretty sure that kid might just pop out any second, giving us all the fright of a lifetime. That would keep Kellan busy for a while and off my back.

Wincing at the pain shooting through my leg, I take in the scene before me.

Camping tables are being set up, chairs are being moved around, and the smell of fresh casseroles, gravy, and grilled stuff wafts over. Someone's even hanging up lanterns, meaning the gang's not about to leave anytime soon.

What the fuck!

As much as I want to shoo my family away, I can't, because I know they're doing this for me.

"I never asked for a fucking party," I mumble to Kellan.

"In that case you should have answered the damn phone," Kellan says. "We've been worried sick about you."

"Sorry for not calling in every night, Dad," I say

sarcastically. "I guess I was too busy drowning in self-pity." My gaze roams over all the familiar faces. There's no sign of Erin.

"Where is she?" I ask.

Kellan cocks his head, feigning ignorance. "Who?"

I groan at the fact that he's making me spell it out. "The physical therapist." I make sure to emphasize the words. "Or did you think I was talking about Ava? You know..." I smirk, ready to turn the tables and annoy the hell out of him for a change. "I think your soon-to-be wife likes me. She takes the whole thing rather seriously. Too bad she didn't meet me first. I bet she wouldn't have paid you a second glance."

He shoots me a menacing look. I laugh, which earns me the kind of murderous look that tells me my brother's still so much in love with her it's unreal. The fact that two people can be so engrossed in each other makes me both hopeful and sad.

Hopeful that there's that one right person for everyone.

Sad that I'll never be the kind of guy to let a woman get close enough to me to find out.

"She isn't your type, so stop the bullshit," Kellan says. "Besides, there's no way she would have chosen

J.C. REED

you over me."

"You sure about that?" I wink at him and dodge slightly, just in case he decides to punch me.

Ava must have heard us because she calls over stoically, "That's right, Cash. I wouldn't have. And you can kick and scream all you want, but I'm not going to sit back and watch you sulk. Not any longer. We've tried your approach; now it's time to try ours."

I scowl at her choice of words. I've known the woman for all of a few months, and she's already taking Shannon's place as the family matriarch. Hell, it's worse. She's already taken it, and no one even saw it coming. Noticing the adoring glance Kellan throws at her, I instantly know who's wearing the pants in his house.

"Actually, I wasn't really the topic of our conversation," I call back.

"Oh," Ava says. "Sorry."

"Cash was asking about Erin," Kellan explains needlessly. "Do you know where she is?"

"She's in town. Ryder's taken her shopping."

"See?" Turning to me, Kellan pats my shoulder and gives me one of his fake caring glances. "Your physical therapist hasn't run off. Take a seat, grab a beer and relax." He leans forward, his voice lowering

128

to a conspiratorial whisper. "And let her help you.

"Why would I?"

"Look at it this way, the sooner you finish your physical therapy, the sooner you'll get us out of your hair. With Erin's help, you'll be back to your half-naked dancers and that stuffy office of yours before you know it. She might be a hot little number, but she also happens to be one of the best at what she's doing." He makes it sound like owning a few nightclubs is a bad thing. Besides, my office is far from being stuffy. In fact, it's all mahogany and state-of-the-art—the best money can buy.

I have a penchant for both women and expensive stuff. I could hire the most expensive therapist if I wanted to. But I don't need anyone's help.

Or pity.

"My birthday's not really today, is it?" I watch my brother grab two beer bottles from the table.

"No, it's tomorrow. What gave it away?"

"Obviously, I know when my birthday is. I was just pointing out a fact in case you didn't know," I say dryly.

I take the beer bottle out of his outstretched hand and settle on a recliner as I let my gaze swoop over the familiar faces gathered around my barbecue. Dad seems engrossed in a conversation, but he keeps peering my way. I'm still pissed at him for not consulting with me before hiring Erin, and glare to bring my point across.

Yes, I know I'm acting like a brat, but I can't help myself.

Between Kellan, who has a baby on the way, and my brother, Ryder, who's about to step into my father's shoes as the town sheriff, I can't measure up. I'm just the black sheep in the family, and I can't change that.

So, why bother trying?

The best I can do is put as many miles between us all as possible.

"I can't wait to get the hell out of here and pretend I'm too busy to answer your calls," I mutter.

"Don't forget the text messages Dad's been sending since Shannon's helped him figure out his iPhone," Kellan says, laughing. "We're all aware of your avoidance techniques. We're just too polite to mention it."

I want to point out that it would be even politer to respect my wishes and leave me the fuck alone. More people arrive, and the alcohol begins to flow. At some point, I spy Erin. As soon as she appears in my line of vision, her gaze flies across the tumult. Our eyes connect, and for a second or two, she blushes.

She's been thinking about me. Maybe even about our kiss. My body heats up at the realization that she must have enjoyed it just as much as I did.

My eyes remain glued to her as I watch her greet Margaret as though they've been friends for a while. She fits right in and looks very much at home, chatting, laughing.

Her hair, which is usually tied up at the back of her neck, is flowing past her shoulders, silky soft and inviting. She's dressed in a flowing, chiffon dress that makes her look like a beautiful nymph. I want to brush the shoulder strap aside and press my lips against her naked skin, wrap my arms around her and pull her onto my lap. The material of her dress is so thin, I wonder whether she'd feel just how hard I am for her...and whether she'd be turned on by it.

Then Margaret leaves, and Erin's standing near the grill, the heat reflecting in her rosy cheeks.

Tipping the bottle back, I take a long swig as I watch her laughing with Ava and Shannon like she's known them all her life.

I should yell and send them all home, but the barbecue smells delicious and Shannon's one of the best cooks in the world.

Who says 'no' to homemade food?

"Having a good time?"

I turn to look at my dad who's standing near the recliner, still wearing his uniform. His lined face doesn't betray much emotion, but there's a glint of worry in his eyes. This is my chance to give him a hard time, but he looks beat, like he's had a long day already. Ever since my sister's death, he's had plenty of those and doesn't quite seem to catch a break.

I can't help but think that my injury has only added to his plate.

"Take a seat, Dad." I point at the recliner next to mine and turn my gaze back to Erin, my eyes roaming over her body hungrily.

The recliner groans under Dad's weight. We're a big bunch—the Boyd men. It's always served us well, particularly with the ladies.

"I meant well," Dad starts.

"I know that." I take another swig of my beer and grimace at the pain shooting through my hip. It's the damn position. I need to shift every couple minutes or else I'll end up blinded by pain.

Dad doesn't just save people for a living. He's saved his sons on more than one occasion by getting us out of trouble, and now he's trying to save me again. Only, this time, there's nothing he can do.

I feel bad for all the heartache I've caused him. I

feel bad for adding to those lines on his face, which seem to get deeper with each passing year. And while he's physically still the strong man who used to carry me around on his shoulders when I was a kid, his eyes have begun to tell a different story.

His getting too old to deal with his boys' bullshit.

"I just want to see you happy and healthy. You know that, right?" Dad says slowly. "Your sister would say the same thing if she were here."

I nod because that's all the lump in my throat will allow me to do.

"Your brother's been talking to you about the wedding?"

I shake my head. "Haven't seen him much lately to give him a chance."

"He's afraid you won't come. We all are. It would crush him not to have you at his wedding, Cash. Please, don't tell me you're skipping it. I know you two don't always get along, but..."

The pain's hidden well behind the unspoken reproach. I hate to hurt my family the way I've been doing ever since going pro. But I can't let them dictate my life.

"I will be there. You know that."

"How can you when you—"

Can't stand straight for longer than five minutes,

let alone walk?

That's what he wants to ask, but is too afraid to. What everyone wants to know. Hell, I want to know that, too.

"Go get something to eat, Dad. This is a party, after all." Even though the way everyone seems to tiptoe around me, avoiding speaking about the obvious, it might just as well be a funeral.

Dad gets up. "Your birthday gift is in the garage."

I look up at him and nod. I don't have to ask what it is.

In a weak moment, Margaret already told me what they were planning on buying. The entire idea seemed absurd, at first, but now that Dad's mentioned the garage, I'm sure she wasn't lying.

"Want me to—" my father asks.

"I'm good, thanks." I turn away, hoping my expression doesn't betray the anger I'm feeling. "And thanks for the motorcycle."

"It's not any bike, Cash," my father says. "It's a Harley Davidson. The newest on the market. You were nineteen when you said you wanted one. It was about time I got you one. Once you walk again, you can take it for a ride."

I shoot him a grim smile.

There, another example. Another reminder of

how big of a fuck-up I am.

I'm not completely immobile, and yet that's what they all think.

"Maybe get me another one of those." I hold up the beer bottle, dourly, and watch as Dad gets up to fulfil my request.

CHAPTER ELEVEN

CASH

DAD RETURNS SWIFTLY with my drink, followed by the rest of the Boyd bunch. We take a seat and Shannon begins to place plates and bowls of food on the huge, long table, in easy reach for everyone to help themselves.

My glance brushes over the familiar faces, and I realize Erin hasn't joined us.

"Erin, come over," my dad calls out, as though reading my mind.

I turn sharply to look over my shoulder and

realize Ryder's hands are still glued to Erin's lower back. They're standing a few inches too close.

He's almost leaning into her, dammit.

The thought of him with her in the car, smiling at her, driving her wherever she wants to be, touching her, makes my blood boil in my veins.

I'm not jealous or anything.

How could I possibly be when she's been here for only a little more than a week? But I don't like the fact that she seems to glow now that he's around. All I ever get is a frown.

The thing is, Ryder is single and a player like me. Maybe not to the same extent as I am, but I'm sure he wouldn't throw her out of his bed. There are plenty of other women he could choose from. It doesn't necessarily have to be my physical therapist.

"Hey, bro." I kick the leg of the table to get Ryder's attention. "What's up?"

"I was telling Erin about the harvest fest we have every year," Ryder says as soon as they've reached us.

"Being your usual stranger to Montana, I've never seen anything like it," Erin chimes in, not even looking at me.

My mood takes a dive to new lows.

I set my jaw, then take another gulp of my beer,

then set my jaw again.

I don't like the fact he's trying to warm her up to this place when I should be the one doing it.

I want to offer her the tour, but how can I possibly when I can't walk or drive?

The delicious scent of grilled steak is wafting over as the serving tray is being passed around, but my appetite's just taken a dive, together with my mood.

"Stay, and I'll take you," Ryder says and winks at her.

My gaze rakes over her, over the way her body seems to fill out her dress perfectly without looking tacky. Her hair's grazing the sun-kissed skin on her shoulders, and suddenly I'm consumed by the urge to press my lips against her body and lick every delicious inch.

As though hearing my thoughts, her gaze turns to me and our eyes connect.

The world around us disappears; the chatter of voices fade into nothingness.

I take a sharp breath as a current of energy shoots through me, and my body becomes alive.

"Maybe Cash will come, too. If he decides to give me a chance."

Her words are soft, earnest, devoid of the pity I've been getting from her and everyone else around me.

I stare at her, taken aback by the warmth and the determination in her gaze.

"We all would like that," my dad says. I can feel his glance at me. I can feel everyone's glance, but all I can do is stare at Erin as she's staring back at me.

I want her.

I've never wanted a woman the way I want her, I realize. I also realize that I've been staring a little too long and my family's bound to notice.

But damn, I can't peel my eyes off of her.

"We'll see about that," I mumble, which seems to please her because she rewards me with a smile.

Throughout the evening, I watch Erin take a nibble here and there, all the while talking and having a great time while throwing secret glances my way whenever she thinks I'm not looking.

What I don't fail to notice is Ryder hovering around her like a swarm of bees around honey. Honey—that she is all right, just not his.

What's with women and guys in uniform?

But Erin's not my business.

I set my jaw and look the other way.

Eventually, everyone says their goodbyes. Shannon's the last to leave after clearing the plates and whispering in my ear, "We weren't so bad now, were we?"

I smirk at her. "No, but don't come back."

"You know we can't honor your wish. Tomorrow's your birthday." Laughing, she slaps my arm, and then the last of the Boyd clan's gone.

I close my eyes and lean back, relishing the sudden silence.

Dusk descended a few hours ago. A soft breeze is wafting the crisp air into my face. From the feel of it, it might rain soon. Then again, this is Montana. Our rainy days are numbered.

"You haven't eaten much yet." Erin's soft voice reaches me.

I open my eyes right in time to catch the paper plate she's thrown into my lap before taking the same spot my dad had just occupied.

Her thigh is almost brushing mine. For a moment, I imagine myself squeezing my hand beneath the thin fabric of her dress, riding my fingers high up her thigh.

"I'm not hungry." At least not for food.

"Eat," she says softly but with enough determination to make me want to take a bite. "Organizing something like this was so kind of everyone."

Following Erin's line of vision, I peer at the cooling down barbecue and the twenty bowls of delicacies Shannon and Margaret were kind enough to prepare to "help see us through the week."

"Yeah," I mumble and take another bite. The food is delicious, and my stomach rumbles in response.

"I can cook up a mean bowl of pasta. But boy, does Shannon beat me to everything else. This is nice." Erin points at the strings of fairy lights Margaret hung up all around the trees a few hours ago. Together with the countless lanterns, it looks like a canopy of tiny, glowing stars is hovering over our heads.

Under different circumstances, the whole setting would have been quite romantic. I would have poured us a glass of wine, and we'd be having sex on my terrace before we'd finish the bottle.

But not with the pain constantly flowing and ebbing through my body.

"Your family's great," Erin says. "They're supportive, loving—the kind anyone would wish for."

I nod and push another forkful of food into my mouth, chewing slowly. "I know. The kind you don't have but have always wanted—until you have them and can't get the hell away from fast enough."

She laughs. "They do meddle a bit."

"You think? How the hell did they manage to

march in here without my noticing?" I ask. "And why didn't you stop them? You should have figured out by now that I don't like visitors, and particularly not the uninvited kind."

"That includes me, right?"

Erin's statement renders me speechless for a moment. It is the truth and yet not quite. I want her to leave, but at the same time I've somehow gotten used to watching her in the backyard or hearing her shower running at night.

And then there's also the lounge chair incident. I haven't quite been able to get rid of the image of her on top of me. My dick jerks to life again, the way it's been doing since the first day she arrived here. It's like my right hand is no longer doing the trick. It wants more.

It wants her.

Kissing her has only fueled my wants and needs. Kissing her has made me realize what I have been missing out on. I want her to leave, but at the same time I want her to stay.

"Dad hired you," I say matter-of-factly. "I didn't get a say in the matter. So, naturally, you're staying because of him."

She nods. "Yes, but I want to assure you—"

I laugh. "Please, Erin. Stop with the reassurances.

I know you're good. I Googled you the moment you told me your name."

"You remembered my name and pretended you didn't?" Her brows shoot up in annoyance.

"I had to make sure he hired a therapist, not a dragon." I sigh. "Don't take it personally. People around here don't wait for an invitation. They just show up and meddle in your affairs before you're even aware of your own matters. Dad means well, but he can be a little overbearing."

Her lips quirk a little, which brings a tiny smile to my face. Who knew Little Miss Prissy had a sense of humor?

I try to sit up straight, silently cursing and groaning. Maybe my family's right and I need help to get back on my feet.

I can feel Erin's hand hovering near my arm.

"Don't," I say sharply.

Thankfully, I've found a comfortable position that makes the pain subside, but it doesn't melt away. In fact, it's become such a part of my life that it feels as though it's been with me forever.

"You've been avoiding me since my arrival," Erin says, ignoring my silent invitation to sit down. "You think that's the way to get rid of me. This and being rude, and obnoxious."

"It's not doing the trick, is it?"

She stares at me gravely, then shakes her head. "You think I've never had patients who swear and proclaim their profound hate for me? Well, think again. It's natural to be resentful, to want to be alone in hard times."

"Tell that to my family."

"I can try, but they won't understand," Erin says. "They think what we're doing is like a workout. You train, and you get better. But in the beginning, during the first few weeks, therapy can be very frustrating. It often feels like you take one step forward and two steps back. It's hard, and it's cruel. Most patients want to give up. It might take all your willpower to keep going. When the frustration kicks in, I'm the one who'll help you to overcome it." She touches my arm. "You will walk again one day, Cash, there's no doubt about that. I'll make that path easier and shorter for you, I promise you."

"Okay." I suck in a sharp breath, but not because I'm pissed. In the fairy lights twinkling above our heads, her eyes are such a beautiful shade of blue that I can barely look away. She isn't just pretty; she's something else. Cool and unaffected. Professional and maybe even a little bit sad. It's such a strange combination; strong, and yet fragile.

Unreachable, yet so damn alluring.

"Okay as in 'you'll stop avoiding me, and you'll let me help you?' Or 'okay as in shut your mouth, and move on?'" she asks.

"No." I draw out the word. "Okay as in 'Will you finally stop with the preaching if I submit myself to your care, but only under a few conditions'?"

"Conditions?" she asks, warily.

"You didn't really think I would go down without putting up a fight, did you? I'll need you to get accustomed to my wishes. Come here, Erin." I pat the space on my recliner, right next to my bad leg.

She crosses her arms over her chest, and our eyes connect fiercely. There's a battle in her eyes. It's not like her to follow a man's command, but she most certainly hasn't met someone like me yet.

"I'm not going to repeat myself. Come here," I say calmly and watch her as she slowly gets up and lowers herself next to me, making sure not to touch me. The fact that she's put as much distance as she possibly can between us irks me, but I choose to ignore it, for the time being.

"My father hired you because he thinks I need help," I begin. "I don't particularly agree with him."

She opens her mouth to speak. I hold up a hand to silence her and continue, "This isn't my first injury, and it probably won't be my last. I've dealt with things like this on my own my entire life. I don't want you here, meddling in my affairs. But I assume you need the job, and you don't seem so bad."

"Gee, thanks." She smirks. "That's quite the compliment."

I frown at her sarcasm. "My point is, if I send you away, my father will hire the next therapist. And that one might not be so...agreeable."

Or fuckable.

"Agreeable?" Her brows shoot up, and she licks her lips. Her emotions are written all over her face. She's angry as hell. Offended. I realize my words weren't well chosen, but I need her to know her place.

"This is what I propose. I want you to stop working for my father. Instead, I want you to work for me. As long as you're here, I'm the boss, and you're to agree to my wishes. You do what I want and when I want it." I hold her gaze. "I expect you to respect my privacy and don't let people in unless I've explicitly told you so. Those are my conditions."

She laughs, but the sound is choked, forced. "You can't be serious."

"Do I look like someone who's joking?" My gaze is cold and adamant. "I will let you help me if you let me be your boss. I want this to be my decision, not because my father wants it."

She laughs again. Then she nods. "Of course. I can most certainly do that as long as you agree to let me aid you in your recovery. After all, I have a reputation to maintain."

"On my terms. I decide when and where. I'll ask for help when I want it, not when you or others think I need it. I'll choose the time and the place for therapy."

"Sure. As long as you push yourself. Every single day. And I mean it, Cash. I'll have to insist that we work every single day. I don't like slacking off." Her eyes are two mirrors of stealth, fighting with everything they've got. She's not a quitter; I can see that much. She's not going to try and please me. And I'm sure she won't go easy on me. I can't help but wonder what it'd be like to deviate from my usual prey into unknown territory. Have someone like her in my bed—someone as determined and demanding as I am.

I regard her for a few moments as it dawns on me that Kellan might be onto something. Maybe my father has done me a favor by hiring someone like Erin Stone. Admittedly, my recovery hasn't seen much progress in the few months since the accident.

Maybe having a bit of a challenge right before my eyes is all I need to get back into both the bull riding and the horizontal game.

Get back into the saddle.

Have a woman warm my bed on the way there.

It's a simple recipe for success. One as old as time.

"I'm not into slacking, either," I say eventually. "In fact, I work hard to please."

Erin narrows her eyes at me, apparently unsure what to think of my remark. I shoot her a lopsided smile and progress to stand, groaning as the pang of pain hits me harder than before, making me sway.

This time she doesn't try to steady me.

I know she wants to, but I wouldn't let her.

I need to be in control for a change.

"Erin, one more thing." I turn to regard her. "No fraternizing with the Boyd family. Ryder, in particular. I don't condone my employees hooking up with members of my family."

Her jaw drops open for a second before a flash of anger shimmers in her eyes. Her cheeks turn a bright shade of red. "I wasn't going to. I'm not a slut, Cash. And frankly—"

"I'm glad we've cleared that up," I cut her off. "I expect you in my living room at 8 a.m. sharp."

"But your birthday...?"

"Is none of your business." With that I turn to leave.

"Cash?" The sudden softness in her tone makes me stop. I don't turn to look at her. "Thank you," she whispers.

"Don't thank me yet." I tip my head, then proceed walking.

Her gaze is burning a hole in my back as I stumble away on my crutches, hating the fact that I'm so damn helpless.

Hating the fact that I'm walking away when I should be staying.

CHAPTER TWELVE

ERIN

MY HEART FLUTTERS and my stomach cramps. Today is Cash's birthday, which shouldn't mean anything to me.

But for some reason, I'm nervous.

I want him to have a great day, and yet I instinctively know it will be one more struggle and fighting. His relatives visiting didn't have the soothing and uplifting effect on him I would have expected. Maybe he had other things besides celebrating on his mind. Or maybe he's simply unsocial. Either way, you never know what to expect with Cash Boyd.

With each passing day, I try to rethink my strategy, only to fail again. He's unpredictable and uncompromising, which is the reason why the task at hand renders me nervous.

I'm standing in the kitchen, my old apron tied around my waist, sweat trickling down my back, as I try to complete today's mission. I shift my weight, juggling several things at once. The counter is covered with flour and pots, and mixing bowls are scattered all over the generous working space.

I only register the approaching steps when he's already thrown open the door to the kitchen. Startled, I lift my gaze, and my heart gives a jerk, as though it's about to flee from my own body.

Cash is dressed in worn, blue jeans and a white shirt that hugs his sculpted body. Not even the tired lines beneath his eyes diminish his beauty. He looks so devilishly handsome, my body heats up and my cheeks catch fire.

I feel like a teen in heat, brainless and completely out of control when it comes to my body's reaction to him. It's like I'm reliving high school all over again, only I don't remember ever having felt this way for a man before.

Ever since that damn kiss, I've been imagining us in all kinds of situations, most involving a bed and plenty of naked skin.

Sometimes, we don't even get to take our clothes off...

I clear my throat and take a sip of water in the hopes he won't notice just how breathless his proximity makes me feel.

Luckily, Cash seems oblivious to my thoughts as his eyes roam over the kitchen, taking in the mess, before settling on me, confused.

"Happy Birthday," I say.

I point needlessly at the cake on the counter, my hands shaking a little because this is the first time I'm baking a cake for a man. It still needs the finishing touches, but I didn't anticipate Cash to get up so early. It's barely five a.m., the sky a beautiful shade of red and the air still crisp.

"What's this?" he asks, his brows drawn.

"A cake. I'm sure you've heard of those, maybe even had a slice or two in your life." Seriously, I might not be a professional, but I do think my cake resembles the real thing. Besides, there's frosting everywhere. I'm probably even covered in it. That's hard to miss.

"I've made it for you," I say, in case it's not

obvious. "It's your birthday gift."

His eyes move to me, taking me in. *Really* taking me in, as though he needs to remember every inch of me. "You're baking a cake at four in the morning?"

"Actually, it's almost five a.m. And I started at three. It's not as easy as it looks."

He continues to stare at me, which is slowly starting to make me feel uncomfortable.

What the hell's there to look at?

Eventually, his gaze focuses on the cake, and I can finally release the breath I didn't even know I was holding.

Cash leans forward, his face so low, I can't read his expression.

"Happy Birth," he tries to read.

"It's not yet finished, obviously."

He looks up. "You didn't have to."

There's a soft smile on his lips. It could be my imagination, but I think there's also a spark in his eyes.

He likes my cake.

The thought makes my heart flutter a little bit faster.

"Well, I wanted to." I shrug, as though I've done this countless times before, and it's no big deal. "I love cake, both baking and eating it. Back home, I use every opportunity to cook. My mom once owned a bakery, and as a child, I used to sit in the kitchen and eat all the raw dough."

I don't know why I'm disclosing this information to him. I should keep my mouth shut, and yet I can't.

When he says nothing, I go on, trying to fill the silence. "Did I wake you? If I did, I'm sorry."

"No. I couldn't sleep." His eyes are focused on me, too sharp, too penetrating.

"Is it the pain?" He nods in response. "Why don't you take your painkillers, Cash?"

"I don't like the way they make me feel."

I want to point out that being in pain all the time will make it harder for him to find the necessary motivation for therapy. But I remain silent.

I watch him as he opens a cupboard.

"Coffee?" Cash asks. It's the first time he's offered me something. His half-eaten sandwich doesn't count. I frown when he pushes a button and a panel slides out, revealing a state-of-the-art coffee maker.

"You've been hiding the coffee from me." It isn't a question, but a statement, with plenty of accusation in my tone.

I'm so astounded I don't know whether I should be angry or laughing at his audacity.

I mean, who does that?

"I had to." He's not even denying it.

"You realize I've been forced to drink tea for days?" I shake my head. "Why did you hide it?"

Cash doesn't reply. Keeping his back turned to me, I watch him fumble with the huge thing. Come to think of it, I don't think I would have known how to use it anyway.

"Cash?" I prompt.

He turns around. "I didn't think you would be staying." He holds up his hand. "And before you decide to say it, I know it was childish of me."

"More childish than the fact you've been hiding from me? Or that you switch off my water to make me want to pack up?"

He lets out a short laugh. "Okay. That was really bad. I've been a complete ass to you, haven't I?"

"I would never call you an ass, Cash." I take a step toward him, but not close enough to touch him. "You had a hard time. That's all. But you're definitely a work in progress."

His brows shoot up. "Is that a good or a bad thing?"

"Depends on how you see it."

The smell of coffee fills the air. I expect him to reply, when he closes the distance between us. His hand cups my face, his thumb brushing my cheek.

For a moment, all I can do is stare at his mouth, wondering whether he's about to kiss me again.

Do I *want* him to kiss me again?

Hell, yeah!

Even though he's my—

"You have flour all over your face," Cash says. His voice is so low and husky, he might as well have instructed me to take off my panties, and I wouldn't be more flustered. My face flushes again.

I grab a towel from the counter to wipe my face with it when Cash takes it out of my hand and rubs my cheek gently. The gesture is so intimate that I forget to breathe.

He leans into me, his lips coming dangerously close to mine. The intoxicating scent of his aftershave reaches me. I inch just a little bit closer to him, and my lips part on instinct, wanting him, begging his mouth to conquer mine.

Our eyes connect, and something ferocious, like a hunger, passes between us.

"I lied before," Cash says slowly. "The pain didn't wake me. I smelled your cake and wanted to know what you were up to. I wanted to see you."

"Why?" I croak.

"Because I needed to tell you how beautiful you looked yesterday." His tone is casual, but his gaze betrays his insatiable lust for me. His eyes are ablaze, undressing me with every glance, scorching my skin. My body begins to tingle in response. He makes me feel chosen, wanted, as though I'm the only woman for him. No man's ever had this effect on me.

I want to satiate his hunger for me, even if only for a night.

"I didn't think you would notice," I whisper.

"I often miss things, mostly because they don't matter. You're not one of them."

My throat goes dry. I want to ignore his remark. He's my patient. I shouldn't pay attention to the intimate things he says, and yet I want to know what he means by that.

"What do you—"

His thumb brushes my cheek gently, the gesture cutting me off. "I notice you, Erin. All the time. How could I not?" His eyes pierce into me, cutting through the layers that have been protecting me for years. "I know what you've been trying to do."

"What's that?"

"You've been trying to make me jealous by flirting with my brother. Just so you know, it's working. I didn't want you to know last night, but I'm ready to tell you now."

"You woke up early to confess that you were jealous?" I shake my head, unsure what to make of it. My patients often mistake gratitude for profound love, but they're never jealous. "Is that why you were so angry yesterday?"

"I wasn't angry," Cash says. "I was disappointed that you wanted Ryder, and not me. I was ready to fight for you."

The thought brings a smile to my face. He can't possibly mean it, but his stealthy expression betrays his determination. This is not the kind of reaction I ever get from my patients, and it scares the hell out of me.

"I didn't hook up with your brother," I say. "I needed a ride to town to go shopping. Given that you've locked your car in the garage, Ryder offered. Where else do you think I got the ingredients for this cake?"

"The cake was your idea?"

"Baking a cake for you? Yes. All mine." I catch his surprised glance and laugh. "Margaret mentioned your fondness for peanut butter cake. As it happens, it's my favorite, too."

He eyes me for a moment, trying to decide whether I might be making this up. It's in that instant that his expression changes. The want in his eyes disappears, and it's replaced with something else.

He's cagey.

I can see it in the way he puts some distance—both the physical and emotional kind—by busying himself with the coffee maker.

I don't know what I did to earn this change in him, but it sobers me up.

Silence fills the air as he prepares the coffee and hands me a cup, his expression grim.

"Why would you be jealous, Cash?" I ask slowly.

"I'm attracted to you."

His honesty hits me hard. I've known it all along, but I didn't think he'd be so open about it.

"That's a normal reaction given that—"

His hard glance silences me instantly. "I don't give a crap about your textbook experience."

"I thought we settled that with a kiss? You said it would be enough," I say weakly, fearing his answer.

What if it *was* enough for him? It sure wasn't enough for me.

"I was lying." He leans against the counter, taking the pressure off his hip. My professional gaze takes in the sudden lines of agony etched on his forehead. But sure as hell, he's not saying anything about the excruciating pain he must be feeling. "Look, Erin.

You can't blame me. I haven't been with anyone in a long time. It's not helping that you're sexy and beautiful, and..."

"And?" I prompt, breathlessly.

"And I plan on doing way more than kissing you. Seeing you with Ryder made me angry because I know my brother. He'd ask you out on a date, and you'd happily go out with him because, let's face it, he can walk, and I can't. I know I have no right to be pissed, but hell, I don't like it. This isn't me." He points at his leg. "If only I could walk, you would see me differently, not just as your patient. And I—" He breaks off.

"And?" I prompt again.

"And I would have asked you out on a date first."

I stare at him, at a loss for words, unsure what to make of him. Of us. I've known all along that I'm attracted to him, but I didn't realize that yes, if he had asked, I would have gone out on a date with him.

Patient or not.

Crutches or not.

"Ryder didn't ask me out," I say.

"Yet." A vein on his temple begins to throb.

He's angry, even more than before. I want to assure him that nothing will ever happen between

Ryder and me, but I sense he's only going to continue drowning in self-pity. That's the last thing I want.

But what I want even less is for him to think he has a claim on me.

"I hope you realize you can't tell me whom I can or can't date. I've been hired to work with you. What I'm doing in my spare time is none of your business, even if that involves seeking a bit of fun."

His brows shoot up and his gaze turns a few degrees colder. "Are you seeking fun?"

I sigh, ignoring the need to roll my eyes. "No, but that's not the point. The point is that even if I felt attracted to you, I wouldn't go out with you."

"Because of some therapist-patient rule?"

"No." I draw out the word to make sure he gets it. "Because I promised your father and Shannon that I'd look after you. I promised them that I'd make you walk again. I don't know if I'm going at this the wrong way. I don't know what to do to make you realize you are your biggest obstacle, but I know that I can't force you to start therapy. It has to come from you. You have to want it, so please tell me what to do to help you along."

Cash remains silent as he retrieves two forks and sits down at the dining table, motioning me to do the same.

"Don't you want to wait until it's finished?" I ask.

"No. It's perfect as it is. I like things better when they're raw, naked." Without so much as a glance at me, he hands me the fork. I take it from his outstretched hand and take a seat.

"Cash." My tone is soft, my voice shaky. "Just tell me what you want. Tell me how I can help you because I really want to. Tell me what you need me to do. Just don't make it so hard for me to do my job."

I stare at him as he cuts the cake and then takes a bite, chewing slowly. Eventually, he shoots me a sideways glance.

"This is good." He takes another bite, then looks up and smiles.

The kind of smile that makes me forget my anger and frustration and even the reason why I'm here.

He's sexy. So damn sexy I want to press my mouth against his and let his tongue resume what we started a few days ago.

"You like it?" My voice is hoarse, breathless, heavy with want.

"It's perfection." He takes another bite. "Truth be told, I knew what I wanted before I met you, that being getting rid of you. What I want now is something else entirely. I kiss you. That's all I've been able to think about. You, naked in my bed. Touching you, pleasing you." He rakes his fingers through his hair, his eyes dark, brooding. I try to breathe, but drawing air has become an impossible task, as though there's not enough oxygen for the both of us.

"Cash, I—"

"No, hear me out. I want to get this attraction out of our way. I want to do therapy, but I can't with all those mixed feelings I'm having about you."

"Mixed feelings?" I ask weakly.

"Some are pretty clear." He sets down the fork, and his eyes focus on me with an intensity that seems to set every fiber of my being on high alert. "I want to fuck you, Erin."

"Right." I swallow to get rid of the sudden lump in my throat.

I should be shocked, angry at his honesty. But instead I find myself aroused at the idea of joining him in his bed. I've never wanted anyone as much as I want him.

"I want to kiss you and hear you moan," Cash continues. "I want your pretty hands on my cock. I want everything you can give. I want to make love to you in every bed, in every room, on every floor. I want to know every part of your body. I can't do any sort of therapy before I've had you."

His words turn into images before my eyes. I stare at him, but I don't see the kitchen around us. I see us naked on a bed, with Cash inside me, touching me, kissing me, making me moan his name.

Heat gathers between my legs. I press them together, tight, but the motion does nothing to alleviate the growing need settling within my core.

I want all of this. All of him.

"You want sex before you participate in any sort of therapy?" I ask incredulously.

The question is simple.

The implications involved are not.

His proposition is wrong on so many levels. It breaks every therapist-patient rule. But instead of declining him, I'm considering it.

For the first time in my life, I'm considering breaking the rules.

"I wouldn't put it like that. It sounds like sexual blackmail when it's not. It's an offer to engage in something that we both want. I agree to your therapy if you agree to let me fuck you."

"Okay." I take a deep breath and let it out slowly. "Here's what I propose." My voice sounds alien in my ears, as if a stranger's speaking. What I'm about to say might come back to bite me in the ass. It might make me feel cheap in my mind, but in my heart, it feels right. "We'll start off with a one-hour therapy session this morning. Right now. Once done, we'll see how you feel about it. If after what I'm going to put you through you'll still want to kiss me, then I'll let you."

His eyes meet mine with a challenging glint. Cash Boyd likes to be rewarded. Who would have thought? "What if I want more?"

I raise my chin, meeting fierceness with fierceness. "You'll have to work for it. You'll have to earn everything you want."

My heart thuds harder when he gets up.

My heart breaks when he stops at the door, hesitating. He's about to leave, or is he?

Not turning, he calls over his shoulder, "What are you waiting for? And don't throw the cake out. I plan on finishing it."

As he slips into the hall, a smile spreads across my lips.

My body rejoices at the thought of getting close to him. It's half a victory. The question is, for me or for him?

Either way, Cash Boyd has said yes. I should have

kissed him the first time we met. Maybe we would have been off to a better start.

***

An hour later, I lean back, my body drenched with sweat and nerves. The first therapy session was a success. Maybe not success, per se, but Cash has made some progress...all while groaning and complaining and swearing his way through what I'm sure must have been the most gruesome workout of his life.

He kept proclaiming how much he hated therapy, and how much he used to love his life before the accident. I let him whine while remaining everything he needed me to be—persistent, annoying, and patient.

Most importantly, patient. Because if the physical therapist isn't, the patient usually gives up.

I timed our session for a little over an hour, giving him time to get into his exercises. Just as I expected from someone with his determination, once he started, he kept going.

"That's it for today, Cash." I release my grip on his leg, removing the pressure on his knee pushed toward his chest. "I don't want you to overexert yourself."

Sweat is running down his face as he peers at me, ready to argue.

His muscles are hard from the effort, his skin is gleaming. For the last two hours, I've been trying to keep my professional cool and not roam my hands over his sculpted body. It's worked so far, but my restraint is running thin.

"One more time," Cash says urgently, his grip on my forearm stopping me from getting up from the floor.

I shake my head grimly. The bending exercises, with me working against him, might not look like much, but his joints aren't ready for more. "You think you can keep going because you think you can do it all in one day. But trust me, you need to stop now before you injure yourself further."

"Have you tried this?"

I smile gently. "Yes, but I wasn't in your condition."

"Then you know this is barely more than a stretching exercise. Reserve your bullshit for someone else, and help me get to the real stuff."

The pain in his voice is palpable. It's hurting him like hell; it didn't in the past. He's ignoring the surge of adrenaline and the warning burn in his joints. I can't blame him for wanting to be normal again, but I sure won't let him do more harm than good to himself.

"You'll get stronger with each session. It's going to be hard at first, but you'll get where you want to be. Just give it a few weeks."

"A few weeks?" he shouts. "I don't have that much time."

I'm actually being optimistic. The truth is that it can take longer. But that's not the point.

I sit down, cross-legged, and regard him coolly. "Then you shouldn't have waited this long."

"I want it to be over this week."

"That's not realistic, Cash. You know that." I proceed to stand and pack up my gear, ready to ignore the sudden outburst he's about to have. They all have one, eventually. "It's not easy for me to see you in pain, but you can't rush your recovery. The human body is an amazing thing, but you need to give it time."

"I don't have time," Cash mumbles.

I shoot him a sideways glance. He's restraining his temper, I can tell from his set jaw and the thunderous look in his eyes.

Just like my patients, I'm always tempted to let them go a little bit further, push themselves just a bit harder.

But experience has taught me, this isn't the way.

"Fine. If you don't want to help me, I'll do it on my own."

Cash struggles to get up. Before I can stop myself, I climb onto his lap, straddling him. It's a desperate attempt to make him listen, but one that backfires instantly.

His eyes cloud over and his arms reach around my waist, pulling me down on him. My breath hitches in my throat. My whole body reacts to his strength and need for me.

My hips grind into his, my core coming dangerously close to his hardness. I don't know when that part happened, but I can feel it through the thin fabric of his workout shorts. His hand settles at the nape of my neck, forcing my head down.

Our mouths connect, eager to explore, hungry for each other.

I close my eyes and relish the sensation of his strong grip on me. His kiss is soft but demanding, carrying the promise of more to come—if I only let him.

Fuck!

I can't let him.

Pressing my hands against his chest, I pull back with all my might. He releases me, albeit unwillingly. The lust in his eyes is evident, scorching, making me doubt my decision.

I want him; he wants me. What's the harm, right?

"Erin." His fingers begin to stroke my neck, drawing circles on my skin. "Don't tell me this was a pity kiss."

The idea is so ridiculous, I find myself laughing.

"Well?" Cash prompts. "Pity or no pity?"

"Absolutely not. Pity couldn't be further from the truth."

He cocks his eyebrows.

"I don't want you to give up. But I can't let you go too far," I say. "If kissing you is what it takes to make you listen to me, then, by all means, let's engage in plenty of it."

"That's all? You kiss all your patients to make them listen?"

His hips grind into me. He's so big and hard, I find myself getting wet at the idea of doing it right here, right now. For once in my life, I want to forget about the consequences and just enjoy what I want.

But that's not going to happen.

I sigh in mock exasperation. "I don't ever kiss my patients. You're the first. Engaging in any sexual activity with my patients could cost me my license. You know that."

"Why choose me to break the rules?"

Oh, for crying out loud!

He wants it spelled out and served on a silver tray.

"Fine, I'll tell you just so you shut up." I roll my eyes. "I happen to be attracted to you, and very much so."

No, make that crazy much so.

His lips twitch. "You need to see a shrink, Miss Stone. I've been nothing but a jerk to you."

"If we see this through, I'll probably end up needing to see one. I'll have to share with him all the murderous thoughts I've been having about you."

"Murderous, huh?"

"Very dangerous."

"Do they happen to involve tying me to your bedposts and doing unspeakable things to me? If so, then by all means, please proceed and punish me right now."

Now he's really getting into it. I should be appalled, angry. But as usual, my reasoning doesn't seem to work around him. I want to tie him up and do unspeakable things to him, after which I'd like him to do sexy and unspeakably dirty things to me.

"Maybe later." Leaning into him, I brush my lips against his, once, twice. Each time our mouths connect, a wave of heat travels through me, leaving a tingling sensation behind. I don't have to see it to know that his touch isn't as harmless as it seems.

With every kiss, he embeds himself further into my soul—and I let him.

Eventually, I pull away from him and start to roll up the map.

"What if I want more now?" Cash asks, watching me.

I exhale a long, shaky breath. "If you want more, I'll need to see more effort from you." I kneel beside him but keep a safe distance. "But if it helps, I'm very pleased with what we've achieved today. You should be very proud of yourself, Cash."

"It doesn't feel like much."

"Wait until next month, and you'll think differently."

"Next month?" He reaches for me. I try to move aside, but he's too fast. Before I know what's happening, his hands settle around my waist, pulling me on top of him. I crash against his hard chest. "I want it now. I want you now. I want you in every way I can get you."

Wow. I stare at him, unable to breathe. I don't

know whether it's from the collision or because of the sudden need to give him exactly what he wants.

"I'm sorry, but you have to work for it."

"What if I can't wait?"

"Then you'll have to exert more self-control." Which I hope he possesses, because I sure don't.

I press a soft kiss on his lips, then scramble to my feet, fighting his hands off of me.

"I can't wait a month," Cash says. "At least let me have a taste of you. Let me lick you."

My heart skips a beat.

Holy shit!

I want that. Badly.

I regard him, wondering if he's saying what I think he's saying. My tongue flicks over my parched lips as I take in his hooded gaze and the naughty glint in his eyes. Slowly, a lazy grin spreads across his lips.

"It's my birthday, after all, meaning I expect a gift. The cake doesn't count."

I shake my head. "You'll have to work for it. No sex until we've done at least ten sessions."

I don't know when I made this decision, but it sure sounds like I've made up my mind to sleep with him. Strangely enough, the thought isn't as vexing as the fact that I've no idea how to make it through nine more sessions with him without giving in to whatever he wants.

"You're seriously going to leave me with blue balls?"

"Yes." I sling my bag over my shoulder and head for the door, calling over my shoulder. "Now, clean up. Your guests could be here any minute."

"What guests?" Cash's voice bellows.

I don't turn to explain that his family's stopping by. I don't answer because I don't want him to see my face. He can't see that he's not the only one who's going to be suffering from blue balls, figuratively speaking, of course.

As I take a quick shower, I can't help but wonder what the hell I'm doing.

Nine sessions are going to be impossible to complete.

I should never have let him kiss me.

I should never have let his hands roam over my body like they belonged there.

Because now I know that there's no way I'll be able to control myself the next time he touches me. I've never wanted anyone the way I want him.

This isn't going to end well.

CHAPTER THIRTEEN

CASH

I STILL HARBOR no intention of doing exactly as my new physical therapist says. In fact, I've made it my top priority to make sure she knows I decide the pace at which we're going.

Erin's a hot little thing as it is...particularly during therapy. No woman I've ever met has been as stubborn and angry as she is.

It's been ten days of therapy; ten days of an angry mix between determination and perseverance. Ten days during which I've wanted nothing more than to carry her into my bed and fuck her until she's coming with my name on her lips. That's all I've been able to think about, day in, day out. And it's not helping that she seems hell-bent on headbutting me at every corner. I never realized just how hot a smart mouth is in a woman.

Why can't she just be the help?

Then I would be able to skip therapy and just work my magic to get her into bed. Instead of having my wicked ways with her the way I see fit, she's the one to call the shots by only rewarding me with a kiss whenever she feels I've earned it.

What are we?

Five-year-olds?

That's the thought that keeps my mind busy and my mood at a new low as I call my club in Chicago.

"This isn't gonna work, Cash. You can't give us a new slogan and expect us to create an entire campaign in days when there seems to be a problem with everything, starting with getting a liquor license to getting the interior design done on time," Jack says.

He's my on-site manager and as such, one of the best money can buy. But right now he's not worth the brain space he's renting in my head. I fight the urge to slam my fist onto my desk out of sheer frustration. If I were in Chicago, face to face with the guy, 'no' wouldn't even feature in his vocabulary. I'm slowly losing my tight grip on my employees; I can see it in the way everyone seems to start to slack off, take the evenings and weekends off, cut corners to get where I want them to get.

"Jack—" I take a menacing breath and release it slowly "—get it done."

"We need you here, not just for the opening," Jack says. "People are getting nervous. We're losing—"

He stops in mid-sentence. I know what he's about to say.

Money.

Without the media coverage, without the celebrities who used to run through the doors, we're just another club of which there's a dime a dozen.

In business, four months equal four years. Right after the accident, the media was in a frenzy, speculating, predicting the worst. Everyone began to feel sorry for me, and my reputation as the super stud—*Forbes* 100 Most Eligible Bachelors of the Year—was in tatters. It didn't help that the accident happened at the same time I noticed inconsistencies in my financial reports.

In fact, my accident couldn't have happened at a

worse time. The clubs' profits began to tank together with my reputation. Worst of all, the competition stole plans, concepts, ideas, and opened a club that resembles mine a little too much.

An irony, too, that they named their little organization Club 99.

I don't need Jack or my assistant or anyone out there to tell me where I need to be this instant.

"I'll be there as soon as I can," I mutter, even though we both know it's not true. This accident has turned me into a prisoner in my own house; a shell of my old self. And no doctor or therapist or friend can do anything about it.

The only person who makes me feel half alive is Erin. She's trying hard to make me feel better. She's trying even harder to pretend nothing happened last week at the party.

But I know myself. I'm an asshole inside and out, which is why I'm not going to let her forget that she wanted me just as much as I wanted her.

A part of me feels bad for using her. Another part of me is pissed off that she's only agreed to sleep with me if I complete her therapy plan, and only if she sees progress.

It's all about her reputation.

The thought angers me.

I've reached the point where only work will be able to relieve some of the tension I'm feeling. After an online conference with the entire team, Jack and I go through last month's figures one more time, and then I end the call, my mood grimmer than ever before.

"Cash?" Erin's voice carries over from somewhere outside.

I peer at my watch. The physical therapy session was supposed to start an hour ago. I kept her waiting again. Usually, I wouldn't care less, but she's stuck around for longer than anyone before her.

She's put up with my foul mood that she deserves credit for her perseverance. She also deserves a clearer message that whatever happens in my life, happens on my terms.

Groaning from the effort, I lift my body off the chair and head out into the backyard. Granted, right after therapy I noticed an improvement in mobility. Maybe it's just my imagination, but I'm sure the pain's a little less intense than before. By the time I've reached the porch, my back is drenched in sweat and Erin is long gone.

I head back inside, ready to wait.

The thought of doing another therapy session with her causes me discomfort.

I can barely get through an hour with her without touching her, let alone days or weeks.

What did she think would happen? That I would happily oblige while keeping my hands off of her?

CHAPTER FOURTEEN

ERIN

CASH IS CASH.

I wish I had believed Shannon when she claimed that you couldn't win a fight with him.

I stare at my image in the bathroom mirror as I prepare myself for what I'm pretty sure will be yet another day without seeing Cash or making the kind of progress I know he's capable of.

Our make-out session happened more than a week ago, and yet I can still feel Cash's mouth on mine. I can feel his gaze on me whenever we're going through the set of exercises I've put together for him. His hands feel hot on my skin as he holds on to me for support. It's those little moments I've secretly come to look forward to.

We've come such a long way, and now he's halting again. He pushes himself, only to give up an hour later. He declares his readiness to participate in physical therapy, only not to turn up.

I begin each day with the same thoughts—will he or won't he let me do my job?

Today is no different.

I shake my head grimly as I regard myself.

Only a few weeks into this job and the dark shadows I used to sport back home are gone from under my eyes. My skin has turned a light golden shade from all the walks I've been taking thanks to Cash's unwillingness to actually let me work hard for my money. I thought we had come to an agreement. I thought Cash meant it when he proclaimed his willingness to work with me, albeit on his terms. I was sure a kiss would suffice to get him motivated.

I was wrong.

Thank goodness I didn't give in and sleep with him on the spot. I wanted to, and maybe, under different circumstances, my decision would have been a different one.

But as things stand, he's too full of himself and in dire need of my help.

And help is the only thing he's getting from me...for the time being.

At eight a.m. sharp, I tried knocking—or rather banging—on his bedroom door...to no avail. I tried calling his name, left a note on the kitchen counter.

Begging, pleading, demanding—nothing seems to do the trick.

All I can do now is wait—again—give him more time.

Minutes. Hours.

Time he doesn't have.

I don't want to say it, but his refusal to work with me is slowly making me frustrated. He's still being difficult even though I've offered him the kind of reward that could make me lose my license.

I want him, but more than that I want him to succeed because I know he can. Unfortunately, Cash doesn't share my confidence in his abilities.

"Maybe I'm approaching this the wrong way," I mutter to my mirror image.

Maybe he's wallowing in self-pity because too many people care, and he enjoys the attention.

A kiss seemed to motivate him for a little while. Maybe I could give him more as we go along until—

My breath hitches and heat rushes through my abdomen, gathering in that private spot that begs for his touch.

The thought of sleeping with him, just for the sake of it, is both scary and exciting. I don't know if I should be shocked or appalled at the fact that I want him to the extent of putting professionalism aside, even though I should know better than that.

Clearly, I need to straighten my head before this job turns into a disaster.

As I change from my usual work attire into tight shorts and a tank top, I devise a new battle plan, one that involves calling Shannon.

***

Half an hour later, I leave my bedroom without my therapy gear, and instead of heading for the living room, I round the house and stroll straight for the open fields and the woods stretching out in the distance.

The broad gravel path crunches beneath my feet. Even though it's barely eight a.m., the air's already scorching hot and heavy with the scent of approaching summer. I take a few long breaths, marveling at the untouched beauty around me.

There's a fence in the distance right next to a huge barn. I head in the opposite direction. It's at least a half-hour walk to the woods, but I have all the time in the world.

Lost in thought, I only hear the footsteps behind me when a tall figure appears right next to me. I jump a step back, and a startled yelp escapes my throat.

"Jeez, you scared the crap out of me." Cupping a hand over my eyes, I look all the way up into the stranger's face.

He looks just like Cash, maybe a couple of years younger. But the resemblance is striking—the same haunted, green eyes, the same dark hair, and straight nose. The only difference is that whoever the guy is, he's sporting a smile rather than the scowl I've gotten used to seeing on Cash Boyd.

"Sorry. I didn't mean to." The guy's smile broadens, revealing two strings of perfect white teeth. "I'm Josh, Cash's cousin. Mom sent me."

"I'm Erin."

"I know."

We head up the path, keeping our stroll leisurely. "How do you know?"

"I know everyone around here." Josh winks. "You're the only new face I've seen in ages. But a very pretty one at that. Joking aside, we've already met at Cash's birthday party."

I narrow my eyes as my brain struggles to place him.

Now that he's mentioned the party, I remember him faintly.

He was the guy who organized some of the stuff—can't remember what it was exactly. There were so many faces, so many people wanting to talk to me, caring about Cash, that I probably wouldn't remember half of them.

"It would be hard to forget someone like you. Want some company?" Josh asks.

"Sure." The compliment is so obvious that I can't help but laugh, and Josh joins in. "I wish everyone would be so happy to see my face."

"You're talking about my cousin," Josh says. "Don't worry about Cash. He can be like that. You don't need the world to like you; it's enough if the ones who matter in your life do."

I nod. "It would still be nice, though. Did your mother tell you why I called?"

"Yes. And she asked me to bring you the blueprints."

I want to say that I've been thinking about invading Cash's privacy because my patients matter to me, but I refrain from it. For one, I don't want to give off the impression that I need to justify my thoughts or actions. And then there's also the fact that Josh seems quite the chatty type, so I should probably let him take the lead. I'm here to help Cash, but for that I need as much information as I can get from whichever source I can get my hands on.

"Take a look," Josh prompts.

I peer at the oversized manila folder in his hand, suddenly unsure. This is wrong on so many levels, maybe even immoral, and definitely not right.

"I'm not really sure I need those. It was just a joke. I—" I brush my hair out of my eyes, realizing my sense of humor wasn't taken as such. I'm already unwelcome in Cash's house. I can't help but wonder how he'd react if he realized I might have gone a step too far by looking at documents that are really none of my business.

"Cash has been disappearing on you? As his contractor I can't tell you why, but I can have you glimpse at the layout of his house." He winks. "Obviously, you didn't get those from me."

"That's—"

"Invasion of privacy?" Josh shrugs. "Sure. But you see, he's pulled the same stunt on everyone else. Someone needs to do something about it." He passes me the documents. "And that someone's going to be you. Just don't mention I gave them to you."

I peer at him sideways. "You said you're his contractor?"

"That's right. I inherited my dad's construction business a few years ago."

I fold the document and tuck it under my arm. "I'm sorry."

Josh laughs. "He's not dead, Erin. Just banging some woman other than my mom. One day he just up and left, leaving us behind. Rather than selling, I took over the business."

I frown.

Josh is around my age.

"You must have taken on plenty of responsibility at a very young age."

His face is focused on the path ahead, his expression unreadable. "Yes. But it wasn't that hard. I've been living here my whole life. I had people who helped me just as I help the people around here as much as I can. It's something we do."

He turns to me briefly, and I notice the strange glint in his eyes. "Cash was one of those people. As soon as he heard that my dad abandoned us, he asked me to remodel his house even though I had no real work or management experience. The house didn't even need a lick of paint. He said he wanted a change and claimed to have been planning to remodel it for a while, but I know better. He wanted to make sure people wouldn't doubt my abilities, and the business wouldn't tank. He helped with my finances and my business's reputation, so I owe him a lot."

I try to imagine the Cash I've known so far taking care of his family. It's a strange image, but it's not completely unfathomable. Maybe he's not the jerk I've made him out to be.

"Anyway," Josh continues. "Business is doing great, and I'm pretty sure Cash's initial trust in me had a lot to do with it."

I smirk. "Your cousin's still one tough nut to crack."

Josh catches my expression and laughs. "Cash is a lot of things, but agreeable isn't one of them. He can be quite a pain."

"Maybe." I smile and look away. I might not be my new patient's biggest fan, but I'm not one to badmouth him either. Josh seems to sense my unwillingness to gossip because he clears his throat, signaling a change in subject is imminent.

He looks at his watch and smirks. "Sorry. Work's calling. Call me if you need anything else. Or drop by at work."

I nod, and we say our goodbyes. Deciding to stay a little longer, I watch him as he returns the same way we came. Once Josh has disappeared from view, I resume walking, his thoughts staying with me.

It's only after I've returned to the ranch that I pull out the blueprints to familiarize myself with the layout of Cash's house.

When I called Shannon, I only wanted to know if she happened to know if Cash had a friend who sneaked him out of the house.

She claimed that he never left the house. And then she offered to send the blueprints.

I peer at the layout and laugh as I realize Cash is one sneaky SOB.

Well, two can play that game.

CHAPTER FIFTEEN

CASH

AFTER MY NO-SHOW for our morning session, Erin's been gone half the day. Not that I've been harboring any intention of doing any physical therapy...not until she lets me do what I want to do when I want to do it.

That she's been gone somehow bothers me, though.

Where the hell is she?

My pickup truck is still parked in the garage, meaning she couldn't have taken it to drive to town.

Not that she knows where the keys are. Her bedroom's empty, and there hasn't been the usual sound of her setting up her equipment.

She's given up on me.

The thought makes me feel both angry and disappointed.

Somehow, for some unexplainable reason, I didn't think she'd leave so soon.

You wanted her to go, remember?

Only, I don't feel the same way anymore because, deep down, this is turning into something else.

I want her...not for therapy purposes, but her, as a woman, in my bed.

Just as I'm about to sit up from my seat in the living room, I hear a door slam, the soft sound of her footsteps carrying down the hall.

Ignoring the pain in my leg, I push up to my feet and hurry out of the living room as fast as my crutches allow me.

"Where have you been?" The question leaves my mouth before I can stop it. There's also reproach in my tone, which she instantly picks up on.

Her brows shoot up. "I'm sorry?"

"You weren't here." Shit. I don't mean to sound accusing and *needy*.

"I'm glad you noticed that, Mr. Boyd." Her jaw

sets.

I want to ask where she's been but the victorious glint in her eyes keeps me back. "I didn't miss you or something," I mumble, digging myself an even bigger hole. "I just thought you had left and that you hadn't even said goodbye."

Her brows shoot up. "You'd want me to say goodbye?"

"No. I'd want to make sure you don't leave anything of yours here so I can lock the door behind you." Her eyes narrow at my remark and I cringe inwardly at my harsh choice of words.

"Good one." She seems hurt, but then again it might just be my imagination.

I don't know why I'm lying, but for some reason, I don't want her to know that, yes, I did miss her.

"I'll be happy to lock the door behind me, seeing that you won't be able to do it yourself. Have a good day." With that, Erin walks away. A few seconds later, a door slams.

Damn!

That didn't go particularly well.

What is it with this woman and her ability to infuriate me with every word?

We haven't even exchanged more than a couple sentences today, and already we're at each other's throats—again.

I bet Dad only hired her to piss me off, and she's doing a great job at that.

It's your damn fault. You shouldn't have paid the last physical therapist to leave.

That one sure as hell wasn't as infuriating as Erin.

"Erin," I yell.

I strain to listen for any sounds, but Josh did a great job at remodeling the house and gave it enough acoustic privacy. I'd have to stand directly in front of her bedroom door for any sounds to carry outside...which I'm obviously not going to be doing.

"Erin," I yell again, even though I've no idea why the fuck I'm calling her. I don't want her to help me. I don't want her around.

Or do I?

Am I deluding myself?

I want her gone because she shouldn't witness my moments of weakness. Yet it seems as though I've grown used to hearing her in the kitchen or watching her outside on the veranda.

That's all there is to it.

When she doesn't answer, I clamber back to my office and shut the door, switching on my computer.

Work is the cure to anything. Managing my clubs is what I'm good at. That and riding bulls.

"Was," I correct myself.

I pull up a spreadsheet and stare at the numbers, trying to make sense of the figures Jack highlighted for me.

For the first time in years, we're in the red.

I need to get back to Chicago. I need to get us back to the top and then sell. It sounds like such an easy thing to do. If only—

A loud thumping noise jerks me out of my thoughts.

Closing the spreadsheet, I get up and head back into the hall. The sound's coming from one of the guestrooms, where Dad's set up the equivalent of a hospital room. That was right before our big fight and my consequent imposed ban on him entering my house.

Erin's there, surrounded by countless boxes. Busy as she is packing up the equipment, she doesn't notice me standing in the doorway.

"What the hell are you doing?" I peer from her to the boxes and then back to the boxes.

"What the hell does it look like I'm doing?" She stops in her motion, but she keeps her back turned to me. I can see from her tense stance that she's angry.

Nothing new there.

The woman just doesn't like me, which makes her resolution to stay unfathomable.

"I'm packing up and sending the gear back to the hospital because, let's face it, you don't need it. It's not like you plan on bull riding again, or are you?" She's not even trying to hide her sarcasm.

"You can't do that." I take a few steps toward her, moving at the speed of a snail.

She turns sharply, and her big, blue eyes slice into me. "Why not? Did I just hit a nerve? Seeing that you like to feel sorry for yourself and I'm ready to give up, I don't think there's a need to pretend that this isn't a waste of time. Let's face it. You don't need therapy. You don't need me. What you need is just yourself and a secret room where you can hide like the coward you are." She points a finger to the equipment. "You don't need this anymore."

For a moment, I just stare into her eyes, struck by the determination I see in them.

"You can't take that with you."

"Try me," Erin says.

"My father paid for those."

She nods. "I know, which is why I've arranged with the hospital to grant him a full refund. Obviously, you're doing fine without all this stuff, so—" Shrugging, she resumes the packing. "—you're not going to need it."

I know what she's doing. She's bluffing to force a reaction out of me. I should laugh off her effort, walk away, anything but—

"Erin, stop."

Her hands hover in mid-air, lingering over what looks like a sad version of a pair of dumbbells. They look so light that I could lift them with my index finger. It's beyond me why my father thought the weightlifting equipment set up in my basement wouldn't do the trick.

"Why would I? You've made up your mind, and so have I," Erin says, lifting her gaze back to me. I don't like the disappointment I see in her eyes as she resumes packing.

"Please, stop."

"Why?" She eyes me warily.

"Because—" Balancing on my good leg, I lift a hand and rake my fingers through my hair, hesitating.

What the fuck am I going to say?

I don't want to do as she says, but for some reason, I also don't want to disappoint her.

"I don't know what I want." My own words shock me. Hearing them makes me realize just how powerless I've been feeling the past few months. For the first time, I don't know what to do.

"You don't know what you want?" she asks.

For a second or two, we stare at each other in silence.

"Do you want to walk again? And I mean without those crutches," Erin says, resuming the conversation. "Without any help at all." Her eyes are so piercing blue it feels as though she's looking right through me, into the deepest layers of me. "I know you do. I can feel it in the waves of anger that are coming from you. I can feel it in your frustration and your unwillingness to cooperate because you're afraid of failure."

"Don't do that," I bark.

"Don't do what?" She stands and places her hands on her hips, her entire stance challenging me now. "Tell you the truth? I'm sorry, Mr. Boyd, but just because everyone's too intimidated to speak up doesn't mean I am. I'm not afraid of you. I'm not tied by some family bonds to be mindful of your feelings. I don't have to walk on eggshells just because you might decide to kick me out. And I sure as hell don't have to prove myself to you. I've had enough of your antics and have decided that my dedication and hard work are wasted here. I'm not going to stay with someone who doesn't want me here."

"You have nothing to lose—"

"That's right," she cuts me off.

"—except your professional reputation."

Her jaw sets and anger shimmers in her eyes.

I try to take a step forward when a surge of pain shoots through me. My leg feels like it's on fire, the titanium screws buried in my bone a painful reminder of that one mistake four months ago.

"Fine, leave. We can pretend you were never here," I say slowly. "I'm a rich man. I can make it happen. No one will know that you failed just like the others."

"But that's the thing, Mr. Boyd. I didn't fail. You did." She inches toward me and pokes a finger into my chest. "And may I remind you, you've been telling me to go. You've decided to give up. I'm just sick of trying to change your mind." She's almost a head shorter than me, and a whole lot lighter. But her determination makes up for her lack of height.

Well, almost.

She reminds me a bit of those little chihuahuas. They have the personality of a bulldog and you know they can bite off your finger if you come too close, but you just can't help yourself because they're too damn cute.

My lips twitch.

Erin's eyes narrow on me. "What's so funny?"

"You are." I laugh at her fuming expression.

Clearly, the woman doesn't just have a short fuse; she also has no idea how to control it. Too bad I own the lighting match to it and know damn well how to use it.

I clear my throat and wink, barely able to peel my eyes off her full lips. "You're cute when you're angry. Anyone ever tell you that?"

"Don't ever call me cute," Erin says indignantly.

"Why not?" I shrug, mirroring her earlier gesture. "I'm a man who always speaks the truth, and you remind me of a cute little chihuahua. It's probably the reason why you're so good at your job. People like you. They open up to you. You should take it as a compliment. Not everyone has such a talent."

Her face turns a dark shade of red, and her palms squeeze into fists. "Did you just compare me with a lapdog?"

"Your choice of words, not mine, sweetheart," I say.

"My patients respect me." Her tone is menacing, lest I dare contradict her.

"I never claimed otherwise."

"It's only you who's so—" She breaks off,

struggling to find her words.

"Stubborn? Confident?" I offer.

"You wish!" She laughs. "I was going for 'an ungrateful brat'."

"I'm never ungrateful," I say coolly. "You see, I always return the favor, at least twice."

She blinks, taken aback by my remark. I can almost see her brain working as she tries to figure out whether the sexual innuendo was really there or whether she just imagined it.

I grin at her, meaningfully, to help her brain along.

Her face turns a brighter shade of red, if that's even possible.

In that instant, I make up my mind.

In spite of the pain and the fear that I might never regain my full mobility in my leg, I haven't felt like this in months.

She makes me laugh; she makes me feel alive; she makes me forget, if only for a few moments.

I don't want her to go—not yet.

I wince at the sudden realization that I've just changed my mind about her.

"That's it," Erin says. "I can't work with someone who's as sexually harassing as you are. You're getting your wish fulfilled. I quit."

"It's sexual harassment now?" I take another step toward her, my right hand pressed against the wall behind her head. "Let me remind you, Erin, that you made me an offer. Go along with your wishes, and I could have you."

She's fuming mad, her eyes two glowing points of anger. "You started it."

"And you agreed to it, and then took it a step further."

She crosses her arms over her chest, bringing those perky things closer to my attention. "Are we seriously fighting right now? What would your father think? He's—"

"—no longer your employer, Erin. I'm your boss. Remember? You agreed." I regard her coolly. "In fact, as I mentioned before, whatever my father's paying you, I'll double it. And we've already agreed that I decide the rhythm. You're to be available at all times, whenever I want you. Three months, Erin. Whatever we do in that time will remain our business. After those three months, you'll get to leave with a glowing recommendation and the kind of job offers that will pay more than you ever dreamed of."

"What you're doing isn't fair. I haven't agreed to anything yet. But you're not really giving me a choice," she says weakly.

"Your words, not mine." I turn around on my crutches, readying myself to leave. "There's always a choice, Erin. But think about it. I expect an answer by tonight."

She remains quiet as I start toward the hall, but I can feel her scowl on me and can't help but smile.

Clearly, Erin's in shock, but even shock wears off.

"I won't do it," she whispers, the words spoken so low, they barely reach me.

I turn around. "What did you just say?"

"I won't do it. My answer's 'no.'"

"No?" I ask incredulously that she would turn down so much money.

Her eyes narrow again. "No."

So, it's not the money she's after. It's something else. "Erin." I pause to make sure I have her undivided attention. "Did I mention I'm a rich and *influential* man? I can turn you into one of the most sought-after physical therapists or—"

"Is that a threat?"

I shrug. "Again...your words, not mine. I was going to say, 'or whatever it is you want to achieve in life'."

Her lips tighten. Apparently, the woman's bright enough not to underestimate me even though I wasn't threatening her.

"You wouldn't try to harm my career."

"You're right I wouldn't. But I could tell people that you're not willing to see a client's therapy through, starting with the hospital where you work part-time and then make sure the medical board hears of my complaints."

"No one would believe you," she says, her voice barely louder than a whisper.

"Why wouldn't they?" I stare her down. "My name's Cash Boyd. I'm not just one of the most famous bull riders in the world. I'm also an entrepreneur and self-made millionaire. And—"

She holds up her hands and rolls her eyes. "Please, save me your accolades. If I wanted to know who you were, I would have read everything I could find about you on Google. But I haven't because I'm not interested. You could be a poor street musician for all I cared." She blows a stray strand of hair out of her eyes, her beautiful cheeks blushed with fury.

I smile, amused.

She frowns at my smile. "Let me guess. I'm reminding you of a lapdog again?"

"You asked me what I wanted," I say, ignoring her question. "I want you to stay."

"Of course, you do." She resumes packing.

"I'm serious, Erin. I want you to do your job because I know you can."

"Cash." Sighing, she turns to face me again. "You want me to stay to do what, exactly? Because you sure as hell don't want me to do my job. I can't work with someone who doesn't want my help. I can't stand back and watch you ruining your health. I'm done with it. Whatever you claim to want today, we both know come tomorrow you'll have changed your mind. Apparently, you don't have what it takes to see this through. Not because you can't do it, but because you're too proud to let someone else take charge for a while. Trust me, I'm doing us both a favor by leaving."

"I'll be there."

"Oh, please." She rolls her eyes again.

"I mean it."

She stares at me in silence, assessing me, trying to read my expression. Seconds pass. Eventually, she shakes her head. "I'm sorry, but I don't believe you. Feel free to give me a bad recommendation or ruin my career. I don't care. My mind's made up."

She doesn't wait for my answer. Instead of resuming packing up the equipment, she slings her handbag over her shoulder and points to the scattered stuff. "I'll pick up the rest tomorrow."

I follow her as she heads out into the hall. "Where are you going?"

"Hotel. We both need to cool off."

I follow her, trying to keep up with her hasty pace, but she's too fast for me. I reach the entrance in time to see her cross the front yard and climb into the tractor Margaret often uses.

"What the hell do you think you're doing, Erin?" I shout.

"What does it look like?" She starts the engine. "Goodbye, Cash."

I want to ask her whether she even knows how to drive the thing when the engine sputters to life, and with a strong jerk pushes forward, throwing Erin out.

My body freezes on the spot as I watch her landing on the ground with a loud thud.

My heart stops as I watch the machine act up—something it's been doing for months. The engine sputters again, then jerks toward Erin.

A rush of adrenaline surges through me at the realization that if she doesn't move from the spot, she'll be run over.

She'll be seriously hurt.

I have to save her. That's the only coherent thought I can form.

Moving the fastest I've ever moved since the accident, I lunge forward.

CHAPTER SIXTEEN

CASH

"ERIN." MY VOICE slices through the air, cutting through the roaring sound of the ancient engine.

She's not moving. She's not reacting in any way. The tractor moves closer to her.

"Get up," I shout and surge forward, oblivious to the blinding pain shooting through my body. It seems the damn crutches are slowing me down more than usual. My gaze switches between Erin and the beast of a vehicle, as I push my muscles to the limit. My arms are burning from the effort and my back is drenched in sweat.

It feels like an eternity before I reach her. As I peer at her unmoving body, fear grips hold of me.

What if she's dead?

I could never forgive myself. Guilt and anger flash through my mind, fighting against each other in equal measure. It was a stupid move to send her away. It was an even more stupid move to coerce her into being intimate with me. That one was sure as hell going to backfire.

I should have stopped her from leaving rather than play games with her.

Push and pull.

I should have never given her reason to lose hope.

In slow motion, I watch the tractor moving toward us. There isn't enough time to get away, not on those damn crutches. I don't care if I get hurt, but I couldn't bear the thought of anything happening to her.

With a silent promise on my lips that I'll do what she wants from now on, I reach out for her, pressing her body against mine. I pull us both out of the way a moment before the tractor rolls over the spot she's just occupied.

Pressing Erin hard against my chest, I close my eyes.

A loud bang cuts through the air and smoke fills my nostrils. Then the rumbling stops.

Her heart beats against my chest. I open my eyes and peer at her, worried.

I saved her. Somehow.

"Erin," I balance precariously on my leg as I brush her cheek gently. That's when I see the wound on her forehead, close to her hairline. The skin's grazed. There's no blood; no swelling. But what do I know? I'm not a doctor.

My jaw sets.

Fuck.

She's hurt, and I'm to blame.

Erin's eyes flutter open, and she peers around her, confused.

"What happened?" She takes in my worried glance.

"I'm sorry," I mutter.

My mouth crashes against hers on impulse, silencing the questions on her lips. I taste her mouth with fervor, savoring every part of it because it's the only way to make me forget the horrific images that could have unfolded if I didn't make it on time to save her.

Kissing her is the only thing that makes sense.

As I brush my lips against hers, I expect her to

push me away, but instead she wraps her arms around my neck. Her body's soft against mine, willing, eager to both give and take.

My tongue spears through her lips as I slide one hand around her waist, molding her to me. Echoing the moan vibrating in her throat, I kiss her with an urgency that takes my breath away all the while thanking whoever's up there that she's alive.

**

Eventually, we return to the house in silence. I instruct Erin to wait in the living room as I retrieve pads and antibiotic ointment. She remains quiet as I treat her head wound, though I can't tell whether from shock or pain.

"We should go to the hospital," I say. There's no swelling yet, but she could still have a head concussion.

"No." It's the first word she's spoken since we got back inside. Her eyes are wide as she peers at me. "It's just a scratch, Cash."

"I want you to get it checked out. Just to make sure everything's okay."

"I said I'm okay," she says feebly.

Ignoring her wish, I call my father, and then I

make sure she lies down as we wait for him. Under different circumstances, I would be the one to drive her to the hospital. The thought makes me angry, and I realize I can't live like this. I can't be helpless all my life and rely on others, not when I haven't tried to change something about it.

The color is slowly returning to her cheeks, but the fact that she's not talking bothers me. I've seen so many accidents in my life that nothing really fazes me. But this is different.

For some inexplicable reason, I seem to doubt my judgment that she will be fine.

I soak a towel in cold water and place it on her forehead, then sit down beside her.

"What are you doing?" Erin asks in half protest, half surprise.

"Making sure your brain's not swelling. It's the only thing I can do," I mutter.

"I shouldn't have jumped onto that tractor."

"This isn't your fault. I shouldn't have made you leave. I'm to blame for everything" I avoid her gaze.

Another thing that I've screwed up. Maybe my family's right about me. Maybe all I ever do is hurt the people I care about.

Erin's hand finds mine and she gives it a light squeeze. "If I remember correctly, you asked me to stay."

I stare at our fingers, the way they seem to fit. I liked kissing her. I like her touch. But more than that, I like her.

"I gave you no choice." I withdraw my hand as I think back to our little disagreement. "I'm sorry, Erin. I know words can't ever be enough, but it's how I feel. I can be such a jerk."

"I couldn't agree more."

I sense her smile and look up to "I wish you wouldn't agree, but I guess I deserve it."

She nods and her eyes sparkle with something that wasn't there before. "Being a jerk doesn't change the fact that you saved me. You made it in time."

"The operative words are 'in time'," I say grimly. "I meant it when I told you that I wanted you to stay. I want you here. I want to do therapy with you, and no one else." I'm surprised by my raw honesty and how much I need her to understand that she can't leave. Not now. Not when we haven't figured out what's going on between us. I can hear the urgency in my voice, the desperation, the distress. I want her to help me walk again. But more than that, I want things to be okay between us.

"You don't really mean it, Cash," she says softly.

"You'll change your mind, and that's why I can't be here anymore. I can't start each day, wondering, guessing. That's just not me."

"I mean it. I want your help." Leaning into her, I cup her chin between my fingers, forcing her to peer into my eyes, into my soul. I want her to feel what I feel. "When you were unconscious, I felt powerless. You made me realize that I can't do it on my own." My thumb grazes her lips, my eyes pleading with hers.

"I..." She opens her mouth in response, and the memory of our kiss flashes before me.

The sudden realization that I need her help isn't the only reason why I can't let her go.

Somehow, at some point, I've grown to like her more than I should. She's started to be in my thoughts at the most unfortunate of times, like when I try to focus on work. I don't want her gone because I fear she won't be easily forgotten.

"Stay, Erin," I whisper. "Stay here. For a while. For as long as it might take."

To see where this might lead, I want to add.

"How can I believe you? One minute you ask me to go, and the next you want me here. How can I trust this isn't just a mood swing?"

"Because this accident has opened my eyes. I was

wrong to send you away." I hesitate, unsure how much I can open up to her. In the end, I decide to go for it because there's nothing to lose. "I've been working out every single day since that damn accident. But I still can't walk."

"You've been training on your own?" She sounds genuinely surprised.

I nod. "With no results whatsoever. Then you came along. After one session, something changed. I felt different. Stronger. I want to continue, but only on my terms."

She grins. "Of course. Your ego wouldn't have it any other way."

"And I still want to fuck you. Nothing's going to change about that."

Her breath hitches.

Quickly, I add. "Not that I expect it. But I want to. And I want you to call the shots. You tell me where and when and I'll be there."

Her eyes narrow. "So, if I ask you to do therapy twice a day, you'll do it?"

"Without a single complaint."

"You better mean it, Mr. Boyd." In spite of the hard edge to her tone, her eyes remain surprisingly warm. "Because I'm sick of your antics. I'm sick of you hiding. And just so we're clear, I know where you've been hiding. That secret room of yours isn't a secret anymore."

I regard her, both relieved that she's staying, and amused at the fact that the woman always seems to know how to put me in my place. "How did you find out?"

"I won't say."

I heave an exasperated sigh. "Now I'll have to kill Josh, which isn't going to be hard given that I don't even like him."

Her brows shoot up. "Who says something like that? He's family."

"Do you have a big family like mine, Erin? Like so big you could probably fill a small village?" I ask, not waiting for her answer. "See, I don't think you do. You only have a sister. Three cousins. Two aunts. One uncle. Lucky you. Nobody's ever bothering you."

"How—" She turns bright red, her beautiful eyes ablaze again. "You've been spying on me."

"No." I draw out the word. "I've only done a background check into you and your family. Given that you were a stranger who basically moved in without my consent, I guess that was to be expected."

"What else did you find out?" she asks warily.

"That you really love your work."

She juts out her chin with pride. "Damn right I do."

"Look." I take a step closer to her. "I'm sorry I was a jerk. I did want you to leave in the first few days, which is why I looked into your background. I thought there might be something I could use against you. But at some point, things changed. I got to know you, and I realized you weren't really so bad."

She crosses her arms over her chest. "Wow, Cash. Your apology sucks. It's even worse than the first one."

"But you're accepting it and we get to make a fresh start. Yes?"

"You leave me no choice, because let's face it. I could have been killed in your front yard. The next time you save me, you better run and fast." Her face remains expressionless, but her lips are twitching.

I laugh and wrap my arms around her waist, drawing her close to my chest. She puts up a fight, but it's a feeble attempt—one that's enticing me even more.

My lips find hers when the sound of an approaching car carries through the open window, the gravel crunching beneath the tires as the driver hits the brake. I release my grip on Erin and peer out at my father.

An instant later, the door slams open. "Where is she?"

"Come on in," I call out to him. I'm in such a good mood, not even my pestering family can ruin my moment.

"We are in the living room," Erin says needlessly.

"What happened?" Dad's voice reaches us a moment before he appears in the doorway, sporting his usual worry lines. "The shed looks totaled."

"I lost control over the tractor," I lie. "Couldn't hit the brakes on time."

Erin shakes her head. "No, Cash. Don't do that. I don't want you to lie." She turns to face my father. "It was me. We had a fight and I wanted to get away."

Dad's gaze shifts from Erin to me and then back to Erin. I can almost see his mind working, probably picturing the scenario before his eyes.

Which is kind of funny.

"You do realize we're grown-ups, right? We don't need to explain anything." I don't even know who I'm addressing.

Dad's gaze narrows. That's when I realize my hand's still glued to Erin's lower back and she's standing too close to me. She glances at me, guilt written all over her face.

So, the woman isn't just hell-bent on revealing every detail that doesn't even concern my father. She's also an open book.

"Outside," Dad bellows. "And wipe that lipstick off your mouth, son. The shade doesn't suit you."

CHAPTER SEVENTEEN

CASH

LET ME TELL you something about my father. I've got the coolest dad in the world. Whatever the problem was, he'd always gotten me out of trouble. Even when we didn't see eye to eye, he supported me and proceeded to meddle in my affairs because he meant well.

He always showed at least some understanding...right after giving me an earful of whatever he had to say.

I sense this is one of those times.

His cheeks are flushed red with anger, his gaze is stony, which is kind of frightening. I mean, the guy's a cop and carries a gun. His fists are clenching and unclenching. His whole body's tense, but his tone is surprisingly calm as he speaks. "You are screwing your physical therapist."

I know better than to trust that tone of his when his posture says it all.

He's about to bite my head off.

My dad's just lost the cool dad of the year award.

This is going to be fun.

"I..."

He cuts me off "Cash." That tone of his is supposed to make me feel like I'm still a teen. He must have missed the fact that I'm twenty-eight years old. "What the hell were you thinking?"

"Relax, Dad. Nothing happened." I grin, which is sort of belying my assurance. But hell, I can't help myself. Winding him up is even better than winding up Erin.

They both have that short fuse thing going for them, but Dad can take it to a whole new level.

"You expect me to believe you?" He cocks his head to the side, regarding me with an air of incredulity. "I saw the glance you two exchanged."

I meet his gaze with a cold stare. "What glance?"

"Don't play stupid with me, boy."

"You don't think it was because you kind of barged in without so much as knocking and you kind of startled us?" I sigh. "But if you must know our private business, Erin and I kissed."

He shoots me a look of disapproval...and then more incredulity. "I'm not screwing her," I say slowly.

Yet.

"I'm disappointed in you." His eyes bore into me. "I leave you alone for what? A few weeks? And what happens? It's bad enough you risk your life for nothing and screw women over at every corner. But does it need to happen in your home? With her? Goddammit, Cash." He gives me another deadly stare. "You better get your shit together. I pray for you that she doesn't sue! Because if she does, I promise you won't hear the end of it." He heads back inside, leaving me staring after him, my hands clutching at my crutches, as I mull over his words.

Not two minutes later, Dad returns, followed by Erin.

"I need to get a few things from town," Erin whispers as she rushes past me.

"Keep it in your pants," Dad mumbles and heads for his cruiser, slamming the door.

From where I'm standing I can see Erin peering at me as she heads for the car. I give her a small nod; my lips pressed together. My father gives me another deadly stare before he starts the engine, and they speed off.

For a good few minutes, I stand in the driveway, staring into the empty space.

I'm a businessman, for crying out loud. Making out with the employees is never a good idea. It can go wrong on too many levels.

I know that.

Dad's right to warn me against it. I would never get sexually involved with a female employee.

Only, with Erin it feels different. Natural. Not like a fling, but like something that could take root, meaning I'll have to start treating it like I want it to grow.

***

It's late evening when Erin returns. Dad accompanies her to the door, but doesn't come in. I don't head out to greet him, either.

He's still angry with me.

Big deal. I'm angry with him, too.

Knowing my father, I know this one will blow

over eventually, but he'll probably watch me like a hawk now. Once a friend cheated him of fifty bucks, and Dad ended up holding a grudge for twenty years and counting.

I bet he only took Erin shopping because he wanted to talk to her. I can only hope he hasn't given her an ear full of his opinions in the process.

But just to make sure he hasn't put her off me for good, I've cooked us dinner.

A table for two is set in the dining room, and I've also lit candles on every surface, which gives the place a romantic touch. I've even persuaded Margaret to bake us an apple pie.

The house smells of barbecue, salad, and sweet crumbles.

"What's this?" Erin asks with a frown.

My gaze takes her in, appreciating what it sees. "Take a guess? Want to take a shower before dinner?"

She nods warily as she peers from me to the candles.

"Just make it quick," I instruct and leave for the kitchen.

She returns barely ten minutes later, her skin still damp, her sleeveless top molding to her body.

For a moment, we're both quiet, eyeing each

other, unsure what to expect.

"Take a seat." I point needlessly at the table. She does as I bid and raises her hand to touch the flower bouquet.

"This looks nice. Are you expecting guests?"

"Just you."

Her lips twitch, but there's a glint of pleasure in her eyes. "Shouldn't you have asked me first?"

"I thought it better to skip that part. I couldn't risk you rejecting me." I wink. "Why? Do you have another annoying patient you have to run off to?"

Her smile widens, her beauty striking.

I point to the lavender bouquet. "They are for you. I wish I could have handpicked them myself, but as you can see—" I point at my crutches and smirk.

"Those are my favorite flowers."

"I know. Margaret told me," I say softly. "I wish I could have picked them for you. On the bright side, though, I cooked."

She peers at me, surprised. "You cooked?"

"Just for you." I smile. "You bake. I cook. We're both not half bad. I guess that's a great combination."

Erin falls silent for a moment as she leans forward to smell the lavender, her thoughts far away.

As if a fragment of her past has captured her.

I wish I knew what she was thinking.

"Erin?" I prompt.

She peers up at me, her eyes glazed over. That's when I notice the small bruise hidden beneath her hairline.

"You went to the hospital." She nods in response to my statement. "Did you need stitches?"

"Luckily, no." At my questioning glance, she continues. "And there's no swelling."

"I wish I could have driven you," I say grimly. "I wish I could do a lot of things."

I don't mean to sound like I'm pitying myself because I'm not. But strangely, I want to be able to do normal things for her.

"You will some day."

Our eyes connect over the table and something heavy passes between us. "You still believe in me?" I ask.

"Of course," Erin says softly. "I know it sounds impossible right now, but you will walk, eventually." Her fingers clasp around my hand, squeezing it. "Did you mean what you said earlier? About starting therapy?" Her voice is still soft, but there is an edge to it.

As though she's doubting me.

"It depends. Will you forgive me and have dinner with me tonight?"

She smiles. The flickering candles catch in her blue eyes, making them shimmer like sapphires. "There's nothing to forgive you for, Cash. Words are often spoken in haste. You don't mean them when you're hurting. They may sting like hell, but then you forget about them. Thankfully, actions speak louder. This—" she points at the table "—is nice. I choose to believe you when you say you want my help. Coming from the guy who would have kicked me out of his house if he could, I guess this is a nice gesture."

"I didn't cook because I felt bad," I say, watching her reaction as I decide to be upfront with her. "I want to make a fresh start with you. You didn't deserve the hard time I gave you." I raise my glass. "Here's to you. Thank you for sticking around when you could have given up on me."

***

My dinner with Erin couldn't have gone any better. We talked about Josh, the weather, Chicago. I asked her what her favorite color was (Alizarin crimson—I had to Google it to find out it's a version of pink), her favorite food (fried chicken), and all the places she's traveled. Her job's taken her to a few places, but as it turned out she's never been abroad. We talked about her plans, her dreams.

We stayed away from topics involving the past and relationships, mostly because she seemed keen on evading them. I would have wanted her to open up to me, but she remained cagey.

The thing is, when I looked into her background, I also stumbled across the police report.

I know why she can be as hard as a nail. Asking her about it isn't an option, though. Not until she trusts me enough to tell me about it.

Until then, I'll keep her little secret like it was my own.

CHAPTER EIGHTEEN

ERIN

I HAVE NO idea why Cash has this impact on me. One moment, it feels as though I've reached my limit and I'm ready to leave, the next I find myself compelled to stay close to him.

The man is an enigma I can't figure out. He's practically a stranger, but for some reason, I've never felt closer to anyone in my life, as though we've known each other for a long time. There's something about him that pulls me to him. I can keep my cool around a hot guy, even when said hot guy looks like a sex god. But I find it impossible to keep my cool around him, and not even his crutches can distract from his perfection.

It's not just his looks that do strange things to me.

It's his smile.

It's the way he looks at me, as though the world ceases to exist, and there's only us left.

Even the frown on his face, and the way he clenches and unclenches his jaw whenever he's angry, is enough to send a ripple of sexual energy through me. Which is kind of ridiculous, not least because that's usually the stuff of rom coms and teenage dreams.

I want him to like me. I want our therapist-patient relationship to work out. Yet, in spite of all my attempts to be kind, mellow, understanding, there are moments when I fail to show any of those attributes. Those are the moments when my emotions get the better of me. Emotions that don't even make sense most of the time.

Cash and I are sitting on the veranda, sipping wine, while a soft breeze blows, cooling my warm skin. It's hard to imagine two people sitting in silence, listening to the wind and the sounds of the night, without it getting awkward. But even the silence feels natural with Cash.

He speaks first, his gaze focused on the stars glowing like little diamonds on the distant horizon. "Want a refill?"

Without waiting for my answer, he gets up, leaning on his crutches.

"Sure. Let me help you." I jump to my feet to accompany him because I know he wouldn't want me to do it for him. That's the one thing I've learned about Cash Boyd—never make him think his injury might incapacitate him in any way.

The clock on the wall in the kitchen says one a.m.

We've just spent the last five hours together without realizing it.

I near the rack with wine bottles and frown, unsure which bottle to choose. The thing reaches up to the ceiling and is well stocked.

"What are you doing?" Cash asks when I climb onto a stool. A startled gasp escapes my lips as it starts to wobble.

Cash's grip on my hips keeps me in place before I take a tumble.

My breath hitches in my throat, and not from the strong grip that's holding me in place.

His eyes shimmer green, boring into me.

He's *beautiful*.

Breathtaking.

Unforgettable.

And so deliciously close.

"Cash..." I start, but the words don't quite find their way past my lips. How can I explain what his touch does to me when I don't understand it myself?

My gaze sweeps around me. Everything's spinning a little bit, but not enough to make me nauseous.

That's when I realize that I'm tipsy.

"Are you okay?" Cash asks.

I open my mouth to assure him that I am when I end up leaning forward and pressing my mouth against his. His lips part in response, matching my need. All nerves in my body begin to fire at the same time, rendering me breathless, tingling with sensation. Cash's hands wrap around my waist and he helps me up onto the counter.

I part my thighs to accommodate him as I deepen our kiss.

His mouth devours mine, mirroring my own hunger for him. His tongue slow dances with mine, tangling and untangling.

I'm breathing so hard, my lungs are threatening to explode from the sheer effort to draw oxygen.

But he's the only oxygen I need now.

His touch is all that my body craves.

My core catches fire, and a deep moan escapes my lips. I'm sure if he were to touch me down there, he'd find me soaking wet, and so very ready for him.

It has been too long, that's why I want him so much.

Oh, who am I kidding?

Even if I had been with another man the previous day, I know I'd still want him.

Cash tenses a moment before he withdraws from me, looking as dishevelled as I feel. Realizing that this is slowly turning into something much bigger than a little crush, I supress a giggle.

"Erin," Cash whispers. "There's another reason why I've been hiding from you. I've never felt so attracted to anyone in my life."

I wet my lips and nod, unsure where the hell he's going with this. But it sure feels like a direction I want him to take...just not now.

I want to kiss him. Feel him. I want him inside me.

"It's hard to explain," Cash continues, oblivious to the urgency gathering deep inside me. "But when you were lying on the ground, unconscious, I thought I'd lose you." His hands cup my face, his eyes two bright dots that betray their depths even in the darkness surrounding us. "You've come to mean something to me. I don't know why. I don't even know how. I just know that you're the first woman who's made me feel more...and we haven't even had sex yet." He shakes his head slowly and smiles. "I didn't think it would ever happen. First, I blamed it on not having fucked anyone for so long. But it's something else. Something that scares the shit out of me."

I freeze, suddenly sober as all alcohol seems to evaporate from my veins.

Is this a dream because there's no way he's saying what I think I'm hearing.

"You have feelings?" I whisper.

"Not just feelings. I have this strange desire burning for you. I find myself wanting to know everything about you while feeling the need to push you away so we don't get too involved. I care for you."

Oh.

I blink once, twice. Stupid me for building a castle out of sand only to watch the tide roll in to see it all crumble to dust.

"That's normal." It takes all my willpower to keep my voice controlled, but disappointment still manages to crawl in.

"It is?" He frowns.

I turn to the window, pretending to watch the soft light of the lantern shining on the veranda. Tears prick my eyes, which is such a strange reaction for me. I clear my throat to get rid of the strangled sensation in my throat.

"Many patients develop feelings for the therapist." Usually, it doesn't happen the other way around. But I guess there's an exception to every rule. I shake off the thought. "So far, three patients have proclaimed their undying love for me. Many mistake gratitude for love. It happens."

"Did you get involved with any of them, like with me?"

I turn to regard him, surprised by the seriousness in his voice. "No."

His eyes are hard, demanding the truth I'm more than willing to give him. "Did you get attached to them?"

I shake my head. "No."

My heart pounds against my ribcage, suddenly afraid of his next possible question. He can't ask me whether I feel anything for him, not least because I don't think I could lie.

A soft breeze wafts past, carrying the scent of the nearby woods.

It takes him a long time before he poses the question. "Did you get attached to me?"

This is it—that one moment I prayed wouldn't come. I can't hide from him. I don't want to, but at the same time, I can't proclaim what I'm not even ready to admit to myself.

My chin is trembling, my hands opening and closing into fists.

"I did. I am," I murmur so low I hope he hasn't heard me. "That's why I asked my best friend to step in for me."

His thumb strokes my chin gently. "Why did you decide to stay?"

"She didn't find the idea of moving to Montana particularly appealing."

Cash shakes his head slowly. "Now you're lying, and we both know it. You could have easily found a suitable replacement if you really wanted to. You could also have up and left without so much as a glance back simply because no one could have forced you to stay. Why, Erin?"

I draw a sharp breath to push oxygen into my lungs. "You know why, Cash." My eyes meet his, my gaze imploring him to stop forcing me to tell him the truth. "The same reason I let you kiss me and vice versa. The same reason why I agreed to sleep with you if I saw progress. I feel attracted to you. I'm—"

Falling for you.

I shake my head again and continue, "I want to sleep with you."

Now.

That's all I can think about.

"Why now?" Cash asks.

I hesitate, unsure how to put it. "I've been wanting it all along, but I couldn't give in. You would have stopped therapy once you got what you wanted."

"Maybe." He falls silent, but we both know it's the truth.

"Your assumption was probably correct," he says at last, giving me a wry smile. "But that was yesterday. Today's different. I've changed."

"Changed how?"

"I was bitter and angry at the world, and took it out on everyone around me." His words are spoken softly, but his turmoil is palpable. The idea of him hurting fills me with sadness. My fingers reach out to touch his hand.

He looks up, his eyes burning. There's no smile on his face, but I can see his expression changing.

His gaze shifts to my fingers. I try to pull back, but his hand seizes mine, holding it in place.

"Being with you feels right," Cash says. "You're the only person who doesn't make me feel like I'm only half of what I used to be. The accident opened my eyes and made me see."

"See what?" I ask breathily.

"That I want more in life. A relationship. For things to evolve between us. That I want to get better, and that I can't do that without you." My heart starts to pump as his fingers begin to stroke my skin. His eyes are as wild as a raging fire as he speaks again. "I have a proposition for you."

My chest rises and falls hard, the touch of his hand making me feel light-headed. "Which is?"

"I want to date you, while we're working together." My heart drops to the floor, then starts to gallop like a horse finding its way to freedom.

"We can't date," I say weakly.

Or can we? Do I even want to say no?

"You don't want me, Erin. That's what you've been saying, but wanting and needing are two different things. I know what you secretly desire...and that's me."

I take a sharp breath, unsure how to deny the fact that he's spot on. "Aren't you moving a little too fast?"

"Only with you." He leans forward, his voice

dropping to a whisper. "Fast should be my last name. I see something between us. And it's not just me. I know you can feel it, too. We're both adults here, so why not skip the pretend part, and just date?"

"I don't know," I say honestly. "I'm not sure what's best for you."

"You are," he says. "You are what's best for me, Erin. How about you let me prove to you that I'm being serious, and... just trust me." His fingers trace up my arm, tangling with the strap of my top.

My body heats up in response.

I know what he wants. I know what I want.

My eyes move to his lips and linger there, wondering how much longer I can keep this insane attraction under control.

His offer is tempting, but as a professional, I have to weigh up the pros and cons.

As if sensing my thoughts, Cash adds, "I promise I'll be the most cooperative patient you ever had. Our personal relationship will have no impact on your job. During therapy I'll be completely agreeable."

A snort escapes my lips. "Agreeable isn't a word I'd ever use to describe you." I hold his gaze. "Trust sounds great, but you know what's better? Proof.

You better be serious about this. If you miss just one session, Cash, I promise I'll be gone."

He nods slowly. "You drive a hard bargain." His fingers squeeze beneath the strap of my top. "Proof sounds great," he repeats my exact words. "But you know what's even better? Facts. And results. You'll get all of those and more." Releasing the strap, his fingers find the nape of my back, entangling in my hair. He holds my head in place, hard enough for me to feel the pull, but not hard enough to hurt me.

His strong grip on me is strangely arousing. Everything about this man seems to be.

"You're going to be mine...and mine alone," Cash says slowly.

"What makes you think I'm not someone else's already?" My voice is a strangled whisper, betraying the fact that I want to be his.

"If you were, the guy would be out of his mind to let you go. No man's so stupid." His lips brush against mine. "I want to date you."

I pull up my brows, feigning surprise. "What happened to just sex? Fuck this attraction out of our systems? Reward you for the effort you're putting into therapy?"

"I've changed my mind. I want everything, and I want it now." His eyes are two green pools of lust, undressing me with every glance. "You're too sexy for your own sake, and I'm too impatient to wait. We're both adults here. We can handle being both professionally and intimately involved with each other. You've already said yes to sex, and now I'm going to show you what my plans for tonight are. Let's just say, they involve you a lot. Just say the three letter word."

"You mean 'yes?'"

He shakes his head slowly, his eyes piercing into me. "No, the word is 'now.'"

His voice augments the tingling sensation between my legs, the sexy rumble making me ache for his touch down there.

Now.

Never has a word sounded so dirty, appealing, and pleasing all at the same time.

I want him badly. I want him desperately. I want him now.

I'm both tempted and appalled by my willingness to go along with it, and quick to act on this attraction. He's my patient—it all feels so wrong and yet so right.

Instead of keeping my professional composure I'm jumping right to the fun.

I want him in any way I can get him. I want to

run my hands down his body, explore every inch of his skin as he hardens for me.

So, what's stopping me?

Nothing.

CHAPTER NINETEEN

CASH

A BALMY BREEZE is blowing across our skin, barely cooling the heat coursing through my veins ever since Erin's arrival. We're sitting on the veranda, her shapely thigh brushing mine, her mouth ready and ripe for me.

She knows I want her—I've never made a secret out of it. Now, she's finally letting me have her.

It's only a matter of minutes until I'll be inside her, savoring her touch, her body. Even though my cock's already hard for her, I can't rush this. I want her to tremble with anticipation, to come even before I've buried myself deep inside her.

"Erin." My voice is a deep rumble, conveying my need for her.

For a second, she stops breathing, her gaze focused on my mouth as I lean over her, forcing her to settle back on the lounge chair.

My hands settle on her knees, squeezing her dress up her thighs to reveal the soft, milky skin.

"Cash." Her voice is barely louder than a whimper, begging me—but not to stop. She's urging me on, fidgeting with my belt, eager to speed things along. Her gaze is glued to the strain of my cock. The tip of her tongue flicks over her lips like she's desperate, hungry for it. Under different circumstances, I'd let her suck me into her gorgeous mouth, but I want to make this time about her.

I want to make it all about her pleasure. I want to hear my name on her lips as she comes again and again.

"Not yet, sweetheart." I push her hands aside and kneel beside her, ignoring the pain shooting through my leg. It's not as bad as it used to be, though. Therapy has made everything more bearable. I'm making progress, and she's the one who's gotten me so far.

Grabbing her hips, I pull her to the edge of the lounge chair and hook my fingers under her panties. She doesn't protest as I remove them and spread her thighs wide open.

She's already wet for me, her pussy glistening with moisture, sweet and inviting.

"I've wanted to do this since the first moment I saw you." I rub my finger up and down her slit, spreading her arousal from her clit to her entrance. Her scent reaches my nostrils, and I growl with need. Eager to taste her, I trail my tongue up one inner thigh, then another, then proceed to suck her little nub of pleasure into my mouth. Her back arches and her hips rise, pressing her hot pussy against my willing mouth.

"Hmmm," I moan and lap at her entrance, licking her moisture like it's the most delicious aphrodisiac.

"Cash, yes. Oh, God." Her whimper breaks, and she clenches her fingers in my hair, unsure whether to push me away or pull me closer.

"Don't hold back," I command and dive my tongue all along her pussy, sucking and licking from back to front. She groans, and I begin to circle her clit in response, my fingers joining in the fun, forcing her to the edge.

Her body's responding, her hips rocking with

each thrust of my fingers, writhing across the lounge chair, opening her pussy for me.

She's so close to coming, I can taste it in the juices gushing out of her and the whimper rocking her chest. Every time she nears the edge, I pull back a little, ignoring her tiny protests, driving her crazy with want.

"Please," she whispers.

"Please, what?" I ask, curling my fingers inside her so the pad presses against the front wall of her pussy.

"Please, fuck me."

"I very much intend to do that, sweetheart," I growl and lick harder until I can feel the waves of pleasure rocking her thighs and abdomen. She fists her hands in my hair, pulling me closer, and then she comes.

My mouth is still on her pussy as I gaze at the beautiful woman splayed before me. Her eyes are closed, her lids fluttering, her lips parted. Her pussy clenches around my fingers a moment before she's carried over the edge into a shuddering orgasm with my name dripping from her lips.

I don't let go of her until she's come twice and her body's shaking with the force of it. When she's stopped trembling, I pull my fingers out of her and push up to my feet, squeezing out of my shirt and jeans.

My cock jumps to life, all ten inches of it hard, the tip glistening with pre-cum. Erin's eyes fly open, and her gaze settles on my cock. For a moment, panic shoots across her face. I'm big, but I know how to use my tool to get the most pleasure out of it without inflicting discomfort.

Leaning over her, I pull her mouth into a deep kiss, hard and soft at once, both desperate and possessive. My weight is pinning her down as my mouth claims her mouth mercilessly over and over again, until my head is swimming with her taste, her scent, everything about her. I could do this all day, every day. But my cock is thick and rock hard, asking to take what it claimed the moment it saw her.

Lifting her naked leg, I pull it around my waist and settle between her willing thighs. Her pussy's coated with need, grinding against my length.

I trail my tongue up to her ear and nip at the sensitive spot. She gasps softly, and when she opens her mouth in response, I intertwine my tongue with hers, one hand dipping down to her secret spot where our bodies will soon merge as one.

"You're beautiful," I whisper and push two fingers into her channel to spread her natural lube. "And smoking hot. Anyone ever tell you that."

She whimpers in response, her hips rise, her walls clenching around my fingers.

"I've fantasized about doing this from the first moment I saw you. I've wanted to take you, taste you like no one's ever done before."

"Then do it," Erin whispers. "Do it now."

I smile at her as my thumb zeroes in on her swollen clit. She gasps and moans, and that's when I slide my shaft into her in one slow motion, inch after inch. Her walls tighten, then relax to accommodate me.

Beads of sweat form on her forehead and trickle down her temple, but she doesn't protest. She doesn't pull me back.

"Oh, fuck," Erin breathes and moans. Her hand fists in my hair, and she lets out a strangled cry, urging me on to go as deep as I can.

Slowly, I rock back out of her. Her hips rise to meet me as I thrust back inside, this time harder, stretching her further. Waves of pleasure sear through my body, blinding me with their intensity. With my fingers pressed against her clit, I fuck her hard until her eyes glaze over and she's rendered a moaning mess. Luckily, there are no neighbors close by because there's no way they wouldn't hear us.

Her walls clench a moment before she comes. Hearing my name pouring from her lips, I lose control and collapse on top of her, shooting my seed deep into her, marking her as mine. As I lay back and draw her to my chest, I'm still buried inside her, still connected.

Her heart is pounding against mine, and I realize this feels different than my usual post-coital cuddling.

It feels right.

It feels meaningful.

Like the beginning of something great.

I lift her chin and place a soft kiss on Erin's lips, also realizing that she's not the kind of woman I'll ever let go.

"Feel my pulse," I whisper into her ear and press her palm against my chest.

"Why?"

"Because it tells you the truth."

"What does it say?" she whispers.

My lips curve into a smile. "I'm wild for you."

***

I never believed in obsession at first sight. I still don't. But Erin comes close to becoming an obsession to me. She evokes all kinds of feelings in me, all of them strangely euphoric, all of them surprisingly good.

All of them make me want more of her.

I'm transfixed on her.

That's the correct term.

Obsessing over the girl.

If I didn't know any better, I would say that I'm falling in love with her. Then again, I was never in love before. So how would I know?

Admitting my feelings for her wasn't part of the plan, but her accident made me realize this might be the time to take risks. It was my fault she got on the tractor in the first place. I made our situation unbearable for her, and as a result she tried to leave.

Now's the time to make sure she stays.

I don't want to ruin my chances with her again.

My fingers brush over her cheek. Her skin is soft, kissed from the unrelenting Montana sun. Her features are relaxed. Her long eyelashes flutter a few times, just like they did when she rode me hard and came even harder. Gently, I brush her hair back and then lean forward to press a light kiss on her forehead.

After doing it on the lounger outside, we moved to the living room, where we talked and then explored each other's body some more.

She's sleeping on the couch now, the soft light throwing dancing shadows across her skin, her hair spread out on the pillow. Being careful not to wake her, I cover her with a blanket and then head into the kitchen to prepare the coffee. As the coffee maker's whirring, I check my phone.

There's a total of three messages, all from Sam, one of my oldest friends. And just as expected, the phone rings. Ever since my accident, he's been calling every week, same day, same time, to check on my progress.

Bull riding is his passion and life. Sam and his brother Joe introduced me to the professional side of it. They even taught me a few tricks along the way, which ended up catapulting me to the top of the game.

I answer almost instantly and grimace as the blaring music in the background blasts through the earpiece. There's the faint sound of a voice trying to fight its way through, but I can't make out a single word.

"Sam, get out of that shithole for a minute. I can't hear a damn thing."

The line breaks a few times, as though someone's pressing a hand over the phone. I can picture Sam elbowing his way through some dingy, smoke-filled bar to reach the door. Eventually, the music recedes, and I can make out Sam's voice.

"There's going to be another competition in five weeks." Sam isn't a man of greetings or friendly small talk. He always cuts to the chase, his tone betraying his excitement. "Joe just told me Dillinger will be in Paeroa on the 16th. How's the leg?"

Five weeks?

I grit my teeth. "It's seen better days, but I'm working my ass off to get it back in shape."

"Are you sure it's not too early, because your dad said..."

"Forget Dad. Just because I can't run, doesn't mean I can't ride." I lean against the refrigerator to take the pressure off my hip. "I could ride any bull with my eyes closed. I know it."

"But last time..."

"Sam," I hiss. "Last time, I made a mistake. I lost focus." Silence ensues for a few seconds. "I know what I'm doing. Give your brother the heads up. He can count me in. The 16th, you said?"

The stifling silence persists. I strain to listen, unsure whether I've just lost him, when the music's back on.

"I don't think it's a good idea. There's news going

around that Dillinger killed a contestant last week and that this might be his last competition. They want him off the list and retired."

"That's ridiculous. Dillinger is the best bull they've ever had."

"Maybe," Sam says. "But people have started to withdraw. He's become too uncontrollable, and no one's willing to risk their lives."

I close my eyes for a moment, trying to push the pictures of my accident to the back of my mind. Kellan should never have shown me the damn video. Then again, I would have found it myself and watched it anyway.

"What's Joe thinking?" I ask after a pause.

"Forget Joe. I'm not doing it, and neither should you. It's getting too dangerous."

I open my eyes, surprised. This doesn't sound like Sam at all. "Are you chickening out?"

He sighs. "I'm worth more alive than dead, dude. Now that my daughter's born, my wife isn't too happy about me getting back into that saddle. I have a family to care for. I can't afford an accident like..."

He breaks off.

"Say it, Sam. Don't tiptoe around me like everyone else. Say it. I can take it." I growl. "An accident like mine." I press my palm against the counter, fighting the urge to slam my fist down. "Tell Joe I'm in."

A short pause, then, "Okay. I'll be back from Hawaii sometime next week. I'll send you the details as soon as I have them. Promise you'll give this some thought, Cash. No one expects you to prove anything."

"I don't need to think about it." I end the call, then toss the phone on the counter. It lands with a loud thud.

A surge of anger shoots through me.

Dillinger is the best bull, and they're thinking of retiring him?

There's no way I'll miss this once in a lifetime opportunity. It would be insane. In the nine years I've been bull riding, there hasn't been a single beast as vigorous and robust as Dillinger. He's the best line I've ever come across.

Busy with my thoughts, I start to whisk eggs in a bowl, adding water and pepper. By the time I heat the skillet and pour in the scrambled eggs, I know exactly what I'm going to do.

Erin appears in the doorway, the blanket wrapped around her naked body.

"Can't sleep?" She rubs the sleep from her eyes.

I glance at the clock. It's 6.40 a.m. We've had less

than four hours of sleep, which is enough for me. Back in Chicago, I often get less.

"There's this important seven thirty appointment I can't miss." I wink. "I've run out of excuses for not showing up, so I'd better not be late. Will you have breakfast with me, gorgeous?"

She leans against the doorframe, watching me with an incredulous expression, as if she still can't believe that I'm truly willing to go through with the physical therapy. I wink again, and her face lights up a little. "Sure. Just let me get dressed."

Right before she disappears, I catch the hint of a smile, and I realize just how happy it makes her to help someone else. That's something I've never encountered before.

An hour later, after breakfast, I join her in the guestroom and we start with light stretching exercises. She's a professional; it's obvious from the way she commands me around, getting me to do everything she demands.

It's hard to believe we had sex a few hours ago. Except for a few meaningful glances, and the way her chest rises and falls whenever she touches me, she acts like I'm any patient to her.

She's patient when I feel frustrated, kind when I let out growl after growl of pain, and supportive when I least expect it. With each new exercise, there's a new surge of energy giving me new hope and keeping me going.

I can do this.

I'll be able to walk again.

I'm going to see Dillinger in five weeks.

In spite of the excruciating pain, the session's over too fast.

Erin's packing up when I say, "I want to do another session right now."

She frowns but begins to unpack the equipment. "I wouldn't rush this, Cash. We have to go slow."

"I don't see the need." I shrug, ignoring the throbbing pain, and begin another set of exercises. "The sooner I get out of this house, the sooner I'll have my dad off my back."

She stops to regard me for a moment. I wrap my arms around her waist and place a soft kiss on her nose. "This was great. I don't even feel any pain," I lie.

She frowns at me and shoots me a strange look as we keep at it for another half hour.

"Want to tell me what's really on your mind, Cash?" Erin asks after we're almost done.

It's late morning, and I'm spent. My back is drenched, and my muscles are sore.

"I want to be able to walk again the way I used to. That's all."

She draws a long, meaningful breath. "As long as the pain's bearable. But I think this is enough for today. Now, let's stretch." Her expression darkens. "I want to help you, but at the same time I fear that once you're back to your old self, you'll do something stupid. You've done it in the past."

"I'm not planning on risking my life again, Erin. Not knowingly, anyway." I look away. Guilt as bitter as bile settles in the pit of my stomach as begin my stretching exercises.

We remain silent as I go through the motions with Erin watching my every move like a hawk.

"I don't know about you, but I need a snack. Want to join me?" I ask once we're done.

She nods and joins me in the kitchen, but I can tell from her tense expression that my assurances have done nothing to dispel her worries.

CHAPTER TWENTY

ERIN

"HOW'S YOUR HEAD?" Cash asks, holding out his hand to help me settle beside him. I join him for his mid-morning snack, keeping a few, safe inches between us, mostly because I can't trust my own judgment around him.

After last night, I need to make sure there's still a professional line between us.

"Good, but it doesn't seem to get any rest." I smirk as I peer at my cell phone. "Your family won't stop asking me to join this and that activity."

Cash catches my expression and laughs. "My family's a lot of things. Very strange is one of them. They can be overly welcoming, at times bordering on sickeningly friendly. Sorry, it had to be you."

"Maybe." I might not be one to let people get close to me easily, but I'm not one to badmouth them either. Cash seems to sense my unwillingness to gossip because he clears his throat, signaling a change in subject is near.

"Anyone give you the grand tour yet?"

I blink, confused. "Of the house?"

"Of everything. The house. The farm. Madison Creek."

"If you count driving through on my way from the airport to here, and then from here to the shops, then yes."

"That would be the High Street tour. I was thinking more along the lines of places to hang out on your days off, where the locals do their shopping, which contractors to visit if you decide you might be interested in staying here." Cash winks, and for a moment I'm unsure whether he's joking, being friendly, or flirting.

"I don't take any days off, as you've probably gathered," I say a little frostier than intended. His smile vanishes, which makes me instantly feel bad.

But Cash can't ever get the wrong idea. I can't settle. Won't. Ever. Simply because it's bound to end in tragedy. "But I wouldn't mind having a look around, do a bit of sightseeing," I add to soften the blow.

His eyes light up again. "Well, in that case, I'll take you out tonight."

Oh, crap.

He had meant it when he first uttered the intention to date me. My pulse speeds up at the prospect of putting a name to what we have.

Dating.

It sounds so strange, so unbearably forbidden, given the circumstances, that I almost laugh with excitement.

And there is also the undeniable fact that we'll end up in bed again, which I can't wait to happen. Except....

"I'm not sure I—"

"Relax, Erin. We'll just grab a steak and beer, nothing too fancy," Cash says, misinterpreting my hesitation, and nudges me slightly. "Just two friends enjoying a good meal. I'll get a change from seeing the same walls over and over again while you get to ask me as many questions about Montana as you want. It's a win-win situation, and long overdue." He cocks his head. "You have to agree I was a poor host.

This is my way of making it up to you."

"Sounds good." I smile at him, relieved. Beer and steak—I can handle that.

"I have a few things to take care of at work. Meet you at six?" His gaze seems rueful, almost as if he feels sorry for having to postpone our date to later tonight.

Our attention is drawn to a sound outside as Margaret pulls into the driveway.

"Sure. In the meantime, I'll be outside if you need me."

I get up and hurry to meet Margaret at the door. Throwing a last glance over my shoulder, I catch Cash pulling out his phone. For a moment, our eyes connect, and I catch the odd glance he gives me.

He's anxious, I realize, and I can't help but wonder what's going on. Because there's definitely something he's not telling me.

CHAPTER
TWENTY-ONE

ERIN

WHEN CASH MENTIONED beer and a steak, I assumed he was talking about some casual joint where he usually hung out, which is why I put on a wrap dress. Nothing too fancy, just a cream and brown thing that emphasized by best features without going over the top, and paired it off with flats.

The moment we arrive at the Michelin star rated restaurant, and I see the luxuriously decorated tables and breath-taking décor through the large windows, I realize I should have put more effort into choosing my outfit.

I also realize this is one expensive place.

Waiting for Cash to take the lead, I brush my hands over the front of my dress.

"What's wrong?" Cash asks. As usual, his annoying, observing self escapes nothing.

"I'm not dressed for this." I point to my plain attire. My hair's pulled up in a knot, and I'm barely wearing any makeup. And don't even get me started on the flats that are practical to walk in but don't do my short frame any favors.

"You look gorgeous. Perfect as usual." His eyes drink me in, and for a moment I'm almost inclined to believe him.

"This was supposed to be two friends enjoying steak and a beer. What I'm seeing is the setting for a date."

"Because it's a date." Cash grins, revealing his white teeth. There's a mischievous glint in his eyes. "I didn't think you'd agree to this, so I decided to omit the expensive restaurant part. Now that we're here, we might as well enjoy the experience. They *do* serve steak, albeit only a miniature of it." He winks as though revealing the restaurant's menu could persuade me into wanting to dine here.

"This is too much," I mumble, peering down at my dress. I wouldn't be surprised if people sneered at us and closed the door in our face.

Oblivious to my doubts, Cash's hand finds the small of my back, and he leads me through the revolving doors, whispering in my ear, "Relax, sweetheart. You look stunning in this dress, though you'll look even better naked in my bed."

My skin catches fire under his scorching gaze. I open my mouth to say something when the maître d' appears to lead us to a private booth.

We take our seats and Cash orders a bottle of wine—some sort I've never heard of but apparently will go well with our dinner. As I peer at the menu, I try to ignore the fact that the prices aren't listed anywhere, which can only mean one thing.

The restaurant's usual clientele is confident enough to dine here and peer at the bill later.

Even worse is the fact that nothing I'm seeing sounds even remotely familiar to me. Whatever these people are serving, it seems like they also invented it.

Once the maître d' has disappeared again, I shoot Cash a venomous look across the table. "You can't be serious."

"What?" He shrugs, his eyes twinkling.

"This is so not—" I struggle for words.

What am I supposed to say? That I'm not used to my dates taking me out to restaurants that serve food I've never heard of? That I never agreed to something as lavish as this?

"Relax, Erin," Cash repeats. "Let's have a great evening."

I shake my head grimly. "You're unbelievable. What's the whole point of this? I'm hired to help you. Not to get my fun out of it. Even if I wanted to, this doesn't feel right."

"I want to get to know you."

"And this is the only place where you can do that?"

He shrugs. "Obviously, not. But it's the only place I saw fit for a first date."

"Are you ready to order, Mr. Boyd?" a server asks, appearing out of nowhere again.

I peer up at him, then at Cash, who meets my gaze.

There's so much to choose from I'm sure I'd have no problem finding something to my liking—if only I knew what I was ordering. As if sensing my confusion, Cash says, "We'll take the seven-course chef tasting menu. And get us a bottle of your award winning wine to go with it."

"What happened to our steak and beer? And who's going to drink all this?" I point at the wine bottle we haven't even touched yet, and he's already ordered a second one.

Cash leans back with an amused gaze, his eyes roaming over my body slowly.

"Well?" I prompt. My hands move instinctively to the napkins, eager to find something to hold on to.

"Is my presence making you nervous?" Cash asks.

"What?" I blink once, twice, my brain fighting to come up with an answer. Should I reveal the truth—that I've never been more nervous in my entire life? Or should I lie and risk that he'll see right through me?

"That's a good thing," Cash says, taking my silence as a yes. "It means you're attracted to me."

Which is an understatement. I've been attracted to men before. What Cash does to me is different. It's like his presence is all consuming, heightening my senses, making me want to do things I never imagined I'd want to do.

Like beg him to cut this date short and take me back to bed.

Or invite him into the restaurant's bathroom for a quickie. Given the expensive flair, I wouldn't be surprised to find it furnished with a plush little sofa in case its rich clientele might be seeking a quick tryst of the horizontal kind.

"You're right. I am attracted to you," I say slowly.

More than he'll ever know.

And not just to his body, or his perfect smile, but also to the way he looks at me as, if he genuinely wants to find out who I am. His green pupils dilate whenever he peers at me, and his lips keep curving into a wicked smile, as though his own private movie is playing before his eyes...and it's very dirty.

Suddenly, I want to kiss him.

Take him into my mouth.

I want all of it. All of him.

My hands grab the wine glass. Swirling the red liquid, I try to sound calm and steady as I ask, "You said you wanted to know more about me. What exactly do you want to know?"

His gaze betrays his surprise, and for a second, I fear that he'll ask about my past. And not just the usual generic stuff, but something more personal for which I'm not ready.

What the hell was I thinking giving him carte blanche to ask whatever he wants to know?

"Tell me whatever you want, Erin," Cash says.

"There isn't much to tell," I lie, my hands clammy.

"I don't believe that." His hand reaches over the table to intertwine his fingers with mine. "Help me understand what's going on in that beautiful head of yours. We both know you had plenty of other opportunities to choose from. Yet you decided to come here. What pulled you to Montana? And don't say money. We both know that wouldn't be the whole truth."

I smirk and break our eye contact. "Do they serve stuffed ravioli? I haven't had that in a while."

"Possibly." He squeezes my hand gently. "You're terrible at changing the subject."

"Maybe." I glance at him pleadingly, my insides turning hot and cold. "I've always wanted to see Montana."

"I'm sure. But what's your secret, Erin?"

I frown at his question. "Why would you assume I have a secret?"

"Everyone does." He looks at me for a moment. "What's the real reason you're here?"

I swallow past the sudden lump in my throat. This is the time to tell him and yet— "I can't expose my soul. Please, just drop it."

Cash nods, and then he gets up and pulls his chair closer. His arms wrap around me, cradling me, soothing me. My eyes fill with tears at his unspoken empathy. My head settles against his chest, the material of his shirt soaking up the tears spilling down my cheeks.

I don't want to cry. I haven't in years, but the fact that I'm sitting here with this man, on the verge of revealing my biggest mistake—my biggest failure—tears up old wounds. Because the truth is much more horrible than he could ever imagine. He might not even understand, and the last thing I want is for him to think I'm a monster.

"It's okay," Cash whispers, his deep voice soothing me.

I shake my head grimly.

Maybe everything's okay now, but once he knows my secret, nothing will be the same again. Whatever he sees in me now, will be a thing of the past, a beautiful farce just like everything else I portray.

During dinner, we keep quiet about my past. Instead, Cash tells me stories about his days in college and all the stupid things he has ever done. And I find myself laughing and forgetting, if only for a while.

The service is impeccable and the food delicious. My taste buds fall in love with the King Crab appetizer, the grilled octopus, and crayfish stuffed ravioli. As we leave the restaurant, countless sparkling stars dot the night sky. Cash stops to place a soft kiss on my lips, and as I savor his taste and scent, my heart both races and falls, plummeting into new depths.

CHAPTER TWENTY-TWO

ERIN

CASH HAS MADE it a habit to take me out for dinner, showing me around and introducing me to his friends and relatives.

It's been three weeks since our first night together, and Madison Creek has slowly become my home. People in town were friendly before, but now that I've been seen with Cash on numerous occasions, they've started to treat me like one of their own. What's strange is that Cash and I feel as though we've become a couple—without an official label on it.

He hasn't taken our dating to the next level but his hand is always on me whenever we're in a public place, our fingers intertwined or his lips brushing my cheek casually. Little stolen moments that always leave a tingle in their wake.

People have started to throw us little, mysterious smiles as if they're suspecting that I'm falling for him. On some days, it feels as though Cash is falling for me, too.

I love the solitude Madison Creek has to offer. The pace is slower, more relaxed, which has started to rub off on me. Even my sister and Ally have noticed. But while I don't feel that I'm changing, it seems as though my heart's slowly falling into place.

For the first time in my life, I'm happy.

Truly happy.

I've found a wave of peace inside me that I haven't felt in a long time. I've started to dream of possibilities.

I want this to last.

This Sunday is no different. After our usual morning therapy consisting of stretching and muscle training, followed by lunch, the phone rings and Cash excuses himself, muttering something about work.

The door to his office remains closed throughout the day. It's late afternoon when I return from my gardening. The sun's been relentlessly hot, and I'm eager to cool off.

After a quick shower, I find Cash still locked up in his office, the door ajar.

I barge in without knocking. "You won't believe what I've just found."

He's sitting in his leather chair, surrounded by stacks of paper and five large accounting books. His eyes rise from the computer screen reluctantly, and I notice the black, rimmed glasses.

My heart skips a beat, and a sudden tingle gathers in my abdomen.

They fit him perfectly, almost as good as the tight white shirt he's wearing. It gives the impression that he's shy, not hot-tempered and impulsive.

"I had no idea you wear glasses." My voice sounds oddly hoarse, strangled, what I came in for instantly forgotten, as hot waves of want travel through me.

Who knew I had a thing for guys in glasses? Or maybe it's just Cash who has this strange effect on me. As if on cue, my nipples bead, two prominent peaks straining against the material of my shirt.

"These old things?" He places the glasses on the desk and rubs the bridge of his nose. "I don't wear them often."

"Why not? You look…" My voice breaks.

Sexy.

Obscenely hot.

"Yes?" Cash prompts, brows raised. There's a playful glint in his eyes, as though he's already figured out that he affects me in ways I'd rather not admit.

"Smart," I say. "And bookish."

A bit like Clark Kent—strong and clever and devilishly hot.

"Interesting choice of words." In a few long strides, Cash has rounded the desk and reached the doorway, stopping only inches from me, and I can't help but notice how smoothly he's started to move. He's barely leaning on his crutches any more. Give it a week or two, and I'll replace his crutches with a cane. Give it another month or two, and he won't even need a cane.

I smile, pleased with the progress he's making.

"I like when you think I'm smart. Maybe I should wear them more often," Cash says.

"Maybe you should." I peer up into his impossibly green eyes and regret it almost instantly. He's standing so unbearably close my entire body reacts to him. My breathing's impaired and my heart can't stop racing.

Cash leans into me, his mouth conquering mine hungrily, his hands seeking my body. I moan into his mouth when he breaks off too quickly. "I love it when you look at me like that."

"How?" I breathe.

"Like you want to rip off my clothes and ride me hard."

My face catches fire, and I bite my lip. Is it that obvious that I want him? Damn, I'll have to work on my poker face.

"Maybe those were exactly my thoughts." I pull him to the leather sofa facing his desk and grab his glasses before climbing on top of him. "You've been locked up in here for hours."

"Missed me?"

"Kind of. But only because you're the only entertainment around here." I smirk. "So why do you hate them?" I put on his glasses and peer at him, catching his amusement.

"I don't hate them." He lifts my chin so our lips almost touch. "I'm just not sure I really need them. They look better on you than on me. You should borrow them tonight." His palms settle around my hips, and I rock them gently against his lap, feeling him getting hard beneath me.

My body screams for him, reminding me that it's been hours since he was last inside me. I've never been the insatiable kind, but then again, I've never met someone like Cash.

Pointing to the folders on the desk, I ask, "Aren't you supposed to be resting?"

"Yes, but business is business. Work never rests."

I catch the flash of worry on his face. "What's wrong?"

"We're constantly in the red, no matter how much money's coming in. We've lost millions in the few months since my accident. The numbers in the accounting books don't add up, so here I am, trying to figure out where the problem is."

I blink once, twice. Wow. Millions is a lot of money to lose in a few months. "Don't you have people for that?"

"Of course I do," Cash says grimly. "But at this point, I don't trust anyone. If someone on the payroll is screwing me over, I want to find out who it is. I won't let anyone else do this job for me and risk alarming whoever's stealing from my clubs."

"May I?" Without waiting for his permission, I get up and get one of the folders.

"Sure." Cash heaves a sigh, as though he doesn't believe I'll find anything but doesn't want to argue.

"Before I decided to become a physical therapist, I took a few business classes. Maybe I can help."

"You already do enough here," Cash says.

"I don't mind." I catch his glance and smile. "I probably won't see more than you do, but it never hurts to get a second pair of eyes, right?"

I wait for his nod of approval before I peek at the papers. Cash pulls me back onto the sofa, his hand settling at the low of my back as he draws me close to nuzzle my neck.

"What did you find?" he whispers against my skin.

His hot breath makes it hard to focus, but I don't complain.

I frown as I try to make sense of the numbers. "Find?"

"You barged in saying you found something. What is it?"

"Oh, right. I forgot." I put down the folder and slide my hand into the pocket of my jeans to retrieve the piece of jewelry. "This old chain."

In the light of the sun streaming in, the pear-shaped sapphire stone sparkles in a million facets of blue. Cash stares at it and his expression changes.

"Where was it?" He takes it from my hand to inspect it.

"It was buried in the soil near the barn." I stare at the stone, marveling at its beauty. When he remains silent, I add, "I took the liberty to clean it. I hope you don't mind."

A few seconds pass before Cash meets my gaze, his eyes dark and distant. "It belonged to my mom. My nan passed it on to her. I thought I'd never find it."

His voice vibrates with emotion.

"It's beautiful," I say, even though the word cannot do it justice.

"After we realized it was gone, we spent weeks looking for it." He dazzles me with a warm smile.

"I'm glad you found it," I say softly.

"No. You did, and for that I'm grateful."

His expression grows distant again, as though he's a million miles away, lost in memories. And then he opens the clasp and brushes my hair away from my shoulder. "I want you to have it."

I stare at him, unsure whether I've heard him right. "I can't accept it. It's your family heirloom. It's too personal."

Too everything.

Ignoring my protests, Cash clasps the necklace around my neck and leans back to inspect it.

My hand moves to it, my fingers gently brushing

over the smooth stone. "It should stay in the family."

The corners of his mouth twitch with amusement. "Why? Are you planning on leaving anytime soon?"

"No. It's just—" I suck in my breath, hesitating, as I consider my words. "You might want to give it to someone special."

Like someone you love and want to marry.

Someone who'll stay in your life even after the job's finished. The thought crushes me, but I need to keep it real. Cash will meet that special someone one day. It's only fair that she wear his mother's necklace.

"You are special to me." His gaze falls to my lips.

"I am?"

"Yes." He nods slowly, meaningfully. "You're helping me." The words sting for some reason. I want to be the one he loves, not the one who helps him. "It suits you, Erin," he says. "And I'd rather you have it than it gathering dust."

Maybe for the time being, but not for long.

"I can't—" I shake my head. It's such a beautiful necklace. But it looks expensive, and our future is uncertain. "I can't accept it, Cash."

"You don't have a choice. I want you to wear it."

I nod because I don't want to start a fight. But I know that I'd never take it with me. "Your mom..." I say carefully. "What happened to her?"

"She died from a gun wound." His eyes don't stray from the stone as he speaks. His tone is soft, but his face remains unaffected. His words are spoken casually, as if we're discussing the weather, not an event that likely changed his life.

Okay, I so did not expect that.

All air is squeezed out of my lungs.

There is a long silence. I dare not speak out of fear that I'll break the moment. I know he'll continue when he's ready.

"It was an accident." He drops his hand from my neck and turns to look at me, his eyes a dark green shade I've never seen before.

It's anger I'm seeing. And fear, and guilt.

So much guilt. I don't know what happened, but it breaks my heart for him.

"I don't have many memories of her," Cash goes on to explain. "But I remember the day she died as if it happened yesterday." He pauses to draw a sharp breath, as though to steady himself before speaking about something terrible. "We were young. I was four, and Ryder five. Kellan was seven, which would have made my sister twelve." There is a long pause. "Yeah, that's about right. Carla must have been twelve."

Suddenly, he gets up and walks out into the backyard. I don't know whether he wants to be alone or whether he expects me to follow, so I follow him, keeping two steps behind. The air around us is quiet, as if every bird, every tree is listening. A cold breeze begins to blow. I rub my arms, but not to keep myself warm.

The haunted look in his eyes makes me shiver.

We sit down on a bench, our gazes focused beyond the vast fields, on the dense woods stretching as far as I can see.

"Dad was already the sheriff. On the day my mother died, he left the house like usual. I knew where Dad kept the keys to his office, so Ryder and I stole his gun from its place to play with it in our backyard. We were just a bunch of stupid kids who didn't know that it was loaded or...real. We thought we were cool just like Dad, pretending to be adults."

Fuck!

I can almost see where this is heading, but my mind can't comprehend it.

I open my mouth, then close it again, waiting for Cash to continue, as my heart begins to slam hard against my chest.

"We had other kids over all the time. I can't remember where Ryder was when it all happened, but suddenly all the other kids wanted to hold the weapon. I tried to fight them off when I saw my mom running toward us, probably to check what we were up to. I don't know whether the gun slipped from my hand or whether someone dropped it. All I know is that when it hit the ground it went off and my mom was hit." His eyes narrow, focusing on something in the distance, a memory from the past only he can see. "At first, we didn't know what happened. There was a loud bang, and then there was silence. Everyone was staring at my mom lying on the ground, a lifeless heap surrounded by a thick red liquid that wouldn't stop pouring from her."

He falls silent again. I stare at him, his words echoing in my mind, burning me, twisting inside me like a poisonous snake.

I feel sorry for the little boy who didn't know any better. I feel even more sorry for the adult who's probably blaming himself every single day.

"She was calm. So calm," Cash says slowly. "I remember her telling Ryder to go and bring dad, then her eyes moved to me. As I leaned over her, she took my hands in hers and kept telling me over and over again that she was fine. She told me that she loved us and that she was proud of us. She claimed to be lying on the ground because she was tired, but

I knew better. I knew something was wrong. I could see in her eyes that she was in pain."

A tear rolls down my cheek at the magnitude of his words. I wipe it away, but more follow in its wake.

"When Dad arrived, she was still warm. The first thing I said to my father was, 'Don't worry, Dad. Mom's just sleeping.' I really believed that. I thought letting her sleep would make her pain go away. I was only four years old. Such a stupid kid."

He turns to me, and for the first time, I see the tears gathered in his eyes.

My chest begins to tighten, my lungs fighting for oxygen. But I can't seem able to draw breath. My pain's choking me.

"At that time, I didn't understand what it meant to die. For a long time, my brothers and I were under the impression that Mom was on vacation and that she'd come back. She told us so."

"She?"

"My sister. Clara was the one who carried the burden of my mom's death. She was always the strong one. We'd ask every day when Mom would be back, and Clara would always come up with a story about some road trip. She encouraged us to write letters to tell her what we were up to, the good and the bad things included, and she made sure to send fake birthday and Christmas cards, even gifts, to make us believe Mom was still alive."

"Did it work?"

"Yes." He smiles bitterly. "Surprisingly well, actually. I was nine years old when I finally realized it had been Clara's handwriting all along. That she was the one who always replied to our letters. I'm pretty sure Kellan knew by then, maybe even Ryder. I think everyone protected me, kept me in the dark for as long as possible."

Cash smirks, his face twisting with pain, and eventually a tear rolls down his cheek.

"What about your dad?" I ask gently.

He shrugs. "He took the fact that he couldn't save her badly. He blamed himself for a long time. I think he still does. Once he told me that he should have been more careful where he kept the key to his office, but the truth is we boys used to spy on him. We knew every crevice, every hiding place in the house." His hands ball into fists as he shakes his head. "We were such stupid kids."

"You were too young to understand."

"Still. I wish Ryder and I never got the idea of playing grownups."

"I'm so sorry." My hands reach out to him,

touching him, the gesture meant to convey the compassion my words cannot convey.

Cash nods gravely. "That's life. You say sorry, and then you move on because you have no choice. Even I did. My father never moved on after her death. We've all been waiting for him to remarry, but he's remained true to her. Even so many years after her death he talks about her like she's still with him."

"Sounds like he never stopped loving her."

"She was his life. That's what he always told her." He looked at me. "My mom's death hit us hard, but we learned to cope. After all Clara did for the family, it's a shame she died so young."

My throat chokes up again as I remember looking at the family pictures in the hall upon my arrival. They tell the story of a happy family. They don't show the tragedy and the tears. I had guessed nothing of those before Margaret revealed Clara's story—a soldier who died in a bomb blast.

"It's her I miss the most," Cash whispers. "It's her I have to thank for who I am. For years, she was the light in the dark. She was the one who made sure we grew up okay when my father started drinking. If it weren't for her and Margaret, none of the Boyd brothers would be who we are today."

His fingers brush over the gemstone

absentmindedly, reminding me of his generous gift. "I'm not perfect, Erin. I've made my fair share of mistakes." His eyes meet mine with the kind of intensity that takes my breath away. "You're important to me which is why I'm telling you all this. I just wished you'd confide in me, too."

I blush. "Why would you say that?"

"Because I know you've had a difficult past."

My eyes narrow at his choice of words.

"I've read the report about what happened to your boyfriend," he answers my unspoken question. "I know you're afraid you'll get hurt again."

I take a large gulp of air as waves of anger shoot through me. "How did you—"

"Find out?" He shrugs, as though it's not a big deal. "The police report. I always take the liberty to look into the people who work for me...or move into my home."

Which makes sense. If I were him I'd probably do the same. Besides, it's not like he made a secret out of it. He already revealed that he looked into my credentials. Reading the police report would be the next step to take.

"So you know about my ex." My anger's slowly dissipating, replaced by relief.

He knows, and yet he still wants me. He doesn't

think that I'm a monster. How could he when he doesn't know the whole truth?

"It happened a few years ago. And it's not like it's a secret. His accident made the headlines, and my name was mentioned a few times." An accident that caused his death. "Teen DUI tends to get a lot of coverage. The truth is he was a really good driver."

He looks at me. "Do you think he did it on purpose?"

"What? I don't know," I lie. "He might have been distracted. Maybe something on the side of the road, like an animal or his cell phone."

We fall silent. This is the moment where I could tell him everything, pour my heart out as he did. But something holds me back. I want him to drop the subject. I want all those memories to go away, if only for the time being.

"Do you still love him?" Cash asks gently.

The question comes so unexpected I almost choke on my breath.

"Do I still love him?" I shake my head. "Did I ever?" I turn away, avoiding his gaze. I could leave it at that, but I won't. Cash has told me so much about his life. It's only fair that I tell him something about mine. "I never loved him, but I cared for him." My voice is trembling, the truth too heavy, the burden suddenly too heavy to carry. I've kept it locked inside me for so long that it's poisoned my heart. I need to let it out, even if it means the end of Cash and me.

"He was my best friend," I continue slowly. "We had known each other forever, so it was only natural that we started dating. The day I lost him, I didn't just lose my boyfriend. I also lost a friend."

Tears gather in my eyes again, but it's not the pain that's too unbearable to keep inside. It's the guilt that's weighing heavy on my chest.

"The newspapers described me as this distraught girlfriend, but the truth is I broke off our relationship that day." I feel so horrible I don't even look up as I continue, "I told him that I didn't love him the way he loved me. That I only cared for him as a friend, and nothing more." I draw a sharp breath, but no oxygen reaches my lungs. "I told him that I wanted him to move on, that he deserved someone who loved him the way he needed to be loved." I shake my head. "He didn't take it too well."

"Was it the truth?"

I look at him and nod gravely. "Yes. He was nothing more than a good friend. I tried to be gentle, but maybe I could have chosen my words more wisely. I don't know. For a long time, I felt guilty. Guilty that I didn't return his feelings when I should have. Guilty that I didn't stop him from driving away. Guilty that he died barely an hour later. Guilty that I chose to reveal my true feelings rather than keep my mouth shut. If I hadn't been so selfish, he might still be alive. Who knows?"

"It's not your fault, Erin." Cash pulls me into his arms, cradling me to his chest, his warmth comforting. "Who knows what happened on that road? For all you know, he tried to avoid hitting a wild animal. Or he was so drunk he passed out."

"Maybe," I say, unconvinced. "But I still can't help myself thinking that I could have handled things differently. I should never have broken things off the way I did. He was a good guy. I was too harsh, and he didn't deserve it. I just couldn't help the way I felt. I—" I struggle for words. "—I felt like I was leading him on, and I didn't want that." My throat chokes up again. "He was always driving too fast because, in so many ways, he was a risk taker like you. He's the reason why I became a physical therapist. I wanted to help others, if only to amend my mistake." My fingers move to the necklace. "I can't accept this, Cash, simply because I'm not worthy of it."

"I want you to have it," he says, stroking my cheek gently. "My mom used to say it was her good luck necklace. She wasn't wearing it on the day she died. I wish she had." He meets my glance, and something passes between us. "I want a part of me to stay with you for as long as you want it."

"Why?" I whisper.

"Because I love you, Erin." His words are soft, but heavy with meaning.

For a moment, I forget to breathe. I forget where I am. All I see is a beautiful man who's just told me that he loves me.

After everything I've revealed to him, his feelings haven't changed.

"I love you," he whispers.

"Even knowing everything about me?"

"Yes." He smiles gently. "Nothing could possibly change the way I feel."

"I love you, too, Cash." The revelation makes it past my lips before I can stop it. But it's true. I love him and I want him to know it, even if this won't last.

His mouth lowers onto mine. My arms wrap around his neck as I push my chest against him, my body ready for him. His fingers tangle in my hair, pulling me to him. I moan as a tingle begins to travel through my core.

The sound of a cell phone ringing jerks me out of

the moment. I peel my mouth off of his and look around when Cash reaches into his pocket to switch it off.

"Aren't you going to pick up?" I ask.

He shakes his head, his lips traveling down my neck, his breath hot and heavy on my skin. "It's not important."

It might not be, but the distraction's just made me realize I need to use the restroom.

"How would you know if you're not answering?" I push him away gently to stand.

"Good point." He pulls his phone out of his pocket and peers at the caller ID, frowning. I wait for him to pick up, but Cash just smiles at me, waiting.

Waiting for what?

That's when it dawns on me. He's waiting for me to leave.

"I'll be right back," I say and head back inside, giving him the privacy he needs.

CHAPTER
TWENTY-THREE

ERIN

SOMETHING'S WRONG.

I can't pinpoint what it is, but the bad feeling has been building deep inside my gut ever since I caught Cash's tense stare at his phone. He kept his distance throughout the following therapy session, working hard but barely acknowledging my attempts at lightening up the mood.

I don't know what the sudden change means, but I don't like it.

Maybe Cash is just pushing his own boundaries,

his initial hesitation replaced with a stubbornness that is almost frightening. Maybe he's being too hard on himself, and it's taking a mental toll on him. Doing physical therapy three hours a day, sometimes twice a day, is bound to backfire at some point. I've tried to slow him down, but he keeps assuring me that he doesn't feel the pain, that he's okay. And then he continues pushing as though he's running out of time.

For some reason, I know his sudden obsession has nothing to do with me.

Something is wrong, yet at the same time, I feel like I'm being overly suspicious.

It's not helping that Shannon called in to ask in a not so subtle way if Cash had mentioned anything about bull riding. He hasn't so far, but I can't shake off the feeling that she doesn't believe it. I hung up with the promise to watch out for him and report back to her in case he behaved strange, which apparently he always does after an accident, right before he returns to that passion of his.

Her words have only amplified my worry. As much as I want to pretend nothing's happening with him, I can't shake off the feeling that he's not being completely honest, neither with his family nor with me. I can't help but think that he's doubled his efforts during physical therapy to get back in the saddle.

By the end of the week, I've had enough. I have to get to the bottom of this.

After the evening therapy session, I follow him into the kitchen. His back is drenched in sweat, the shirt clinging to his sexy body.

Fighting the urge to touch him, I rest my elbows on the counter and proceed to watch him as he prepares his usual protein shake. "Ever intend to show me your secret room?"

He doesn't have to show me anything, but I hope he'll open up to me, I only to scatter my doubts. A room tells only so much about a person, but with some luck, I might find a hint as to what he's up to.

Cash downs his drink before nodding. "I'll show you. There's nothing much to see though." He places his glass in the sink and heads out, calling over his shoulder, "Are you coming?"

"Now?"

"Why not? Do you have other plans?"

"No. I—"

"Let's go, then."

I let Cash lead the way, following a step behind. Excitement pulses through me as we cross his bedroom.

I've been in his bedroom countless times, but I never noticed anything out of the ordinary. I glance around the room, unsure what we're doing in here. "So, where is it exactly?"

His hand on the low of my back, the gesture intimate. My breath hitches, and I fight the urge to wrap my arms around his neck and draw his mouth into a deep kiss.

"I'll show you."

We enter his walk-in closet. I frown as I scan the male clothes and rows of shoes.

There's also a suitcase and a black bag.

This isn't the secret room I spied in the blueprints, the one that leads to the backyard. Either he has a second one, or he doesn't want to show me that particular space after all.

He shoves the shirts aside to reveal a large mirror on the wall.

"Look closer." He places himself behind me, his gaze fixed on the image of us.

"What am I supposed to see?" I narrow my eyes. It looks like an ordinary mirror.

He reaches past my shoulder, his lips brushing my earlobe as he whispers, "This."

It takes me a few seconds to see what he's pointing at, but it's there. The transparent circle looks like a logo or a flat screen button—faint and easy to miss. Cash touches it, and the circle lights up blue the same time the bulbs above the mirror switch on. Another press of his finger and the lights go off again. He keeps his finger pressed on the circle for a few seconds after which the mirror slowly slides inward, like a door.

"Not bad," I say laughing.

I peer through the open space at what turns out to be a stairway to the basement. The light is switched on, bathing the stairs in brightness. Cash leads me downstairs into a vast room, and a small gasp escapes my lips.

The place looks like an underground party room with a bar on the east side. The entire ceiling is made of soft blue LED spots that resemble sparkling stars. It's all so familiar. I've seen this before— maybe in a spa magazine and advert for a luxury home. The design is so stunning it takes my breath away.

"What is this?" I ask, unable to tear my gaze away.

"My very own panic room."

"You call this a panic room?"

"There's more." Cash smiles at me and flips a switch. The walls start to gleam blue, revealing a shimmering, ornamental tapestry.

"Is this where you were hiding every time you wanted to avoid me? No wonder you wouldn't come out. This is beautiful."

"It wasn't personal."

I glare at him, but I can't quite be angry. "It wasn't personal that you avoided me or that you wouldn't leave this place?"

"Both." The corners of his lips turn upward. "This is my refuge. Call it my man cave if you will."

"Your refuge?" I roll my eyes playfully. "You live alone and your house is huge." My fingers brush over the tapestry. It feels warm to the touch, probably from the light bulbs behind it.

"This is where it all started," Cash whispers.

"What?"

"The concept for my clubs."

I turn to regard him. His eyes shimmer dark and as deep as an ocean. I can see his enthusiasm for his work, but there's something else, too. "You know I own a string of night clubs, right?"

"Your aunt mentioned it."

He nods. "Good. Then I don't have to tell you that Club 69..."

Club 69.

Oh, wait.

I scan the open space, taking it in with new eyes. That's why it looks so familiar. I recognize the lights, the design, everything. Club 69 is a brand with a website and merchandise. I remember reading something about each club making millions a year, and there are a whole lot of them.

Which would make Cash at least a multi-millionaire. Maybe even a billionaire, but that's too much money to think about.

"You look shocked," Cash says casually.

"I thought...you meant..."

"A low profile club? A bar?" He laughs. "No, sweetheart. I own the Club 69 brand which consists of thirty-eight clubs."

And some of them have been featured in various magazines, which is why I feel like I've seen this before.

"Is that why you're so driven suddenly? Why you've been pushing so hard lately? To get back to work?"

His eyes narrow. "Why else would I work hard? I need to get back to business. Being stuck in Montana isn't exactly infusing confidence in my investors. Why are you asking?"

I stare at the hardwood floor as heat floods my cheeks. "Because I hope your sudden motivation isn't stemming from a need to resume your bull riding activities. Shannon said you'd had various accidents before and yet you keep riding." I lift my glance to meet his hard stare. "Is it true?"

His face betrays no emotions. "What do you want to hear?"

"That you're not thinking of going back to bull riding. You hit your head and survived it. Next time you might not be so lucky."

He shrugs. "That was a long time ago."

"Not long enough, Cash. Your doctors warned you, yet you did it again, and here you are." I point at his leg, then add softly, "You need to find yourself a sports activity that doesn't involve you breaking your neck."

His lips twitch. "I'm very much into physical contact. You know anything that involves a lot of stroking, and plenty of touching."

"I'm serious, Cash. You could have been killed."

"My family's being dramatic." He catches my scowl, and his expression softens a little. "Look, I'm not going back to bull riding, if that's what you want to hear."

"Are you sure?" I cringe inwardly at how hopeful I sound. This is none of my business, and yet it is because I care for him...more than I'm ready to admit to myself.

"No, but it's what you want to hear, right?"

I groan with frustration. He's not taking anything seriously. He doesn't care that his risk-taking is hurting the people he loves. "Everyone's worried about you. Everyone including me. I've read your health report countless times. You can't ever ride again. You need to understand that, but you don't seem to. And now you've started to be weird again, just like before. People say it's a pattern, and it's been making me nervous."

I know I'm rambling, but I can't help myself. His unwillingness to realize that he's risking his life is making me more upset than I should be.

"Relax, sweetheart. I'm..." He's struggling for words, but something flashes in his eyes. "...under a lot of pressure right now. Bull riding has always been my outlet. It's always helped me take my mind off of things. You can tell Shannon to mind her own business, and that I can take care of myself. I know what I'm doing." He reaches out his hand to touch my cheek gently. "But if it means so much to you, I won't do it again."

I bite my lip as I regard him. Did he just say what I think he said? It's so unlike me to get emotional, but I can't help myself. "You'll stop?" My voice is quivering.

"Not a fan of bull riding, huh?"

"It's not that." I hesitate, unsure how to put it so I won't hurt his feelings. "It's dangerous, and unfair to the poor animals."

"The animals?" He sounds surprised.

"Yes. It's cruel. No one asked them if they wanted to take part. They're forced to act aggressively."

His sexy smile stretches into a grin. "You're an animal activist. You didn't strike me as one."

"Why? Because I'm not running around waving banners and shouting for the whole world to hear that I'm a vegan?"

"It's not like that, Erin. I can assure you they treat the bulls with as much respect as they treat the rider. The animals are well groomed, get health inspections, a special blend of food, and they never buck more than twice at a single event. Speaking of food—" He cocks his head. "Did you chuck out your steak last night?"

My cheeks heat up. "I thought you wouldn't notice."

"I didn't, at first." His thumb brushes my chin, lifting it up. "But Margaret asked me why I'd throw away a perfect steak. She offered to feed it to her dogs. It didn't make sense to me. Until now."

"I'm sorry." I grimace, realizing I should have just eaten it because you don't throw away food when people cook it for you.

"Why didn't you tell me, Erin? You've been here for weeks, and you didn't once mention that you were a vegetarian."

"I didn't want to be rude." I shrug. "Besides, I'm not a vegetarian. I just don't eat some animals, like the kind that recognizes you as their owner. Or the kind that is capable of loving you back. That's all. It's the same reason why I don't like bull riding or any sport that involves torturing animals for fun." I stop, wondering whether I've said too much. This might be the moment he'll decide that we don't have much in common, but I don't care. I need him to know who I am as a person.

Cash stares at me for a few seconds. And then he smiles, and I know while we might not have everything in common, at least he respects my viewpoint.

"You promise?" I whisper.

It takes him a while to reply, but when he does his tone is soft. "I promise. Now, let's watch a movie."

He pulls out his cell phone and opens what looks like an app. I want to say more, to thank him for being agreeable, but I sense that might not be a word he might want to hear. So I just keep my mouth shut. A moment later, the lights go out, and the wall before us turns into a white screen.

"Wow. An indoor cinema." I laugh, impressed. "You really know how to take relaxation to a whole new level."

"We haven't even started yet." He leads me to the most incredible high-tech sofa I've ever seen—an oversized circle in the middle of the room, decorated with countless pillows.

"I wouldn't be surprised to find it can spin," I mutter.

"Actually, it can." He laughs at my expression. "Take a seat. I'll be back in a second."

"Where are you going?"

"To make us popcorn." He cocks his eyebrow. "Why? Are you scared I might lock you in here and hold you captive?"

I smirk. "That would suck. No one would ever find me."

"You sure you don't want to leave now, as long as the door's open?"

I drop on the sofa and sigh with delight at how comfortable it is. "I'll take my chances."

He laughs out loud. "You trust me."

I actually do, I realize. Too much, too soon.

"Make it fast, Cash. I want to see that movie." Lying back against the pillows, I close my eyes. Everything smells of him. The pillows, the air. I inhale deeply as my muscles slowly begin to relax.

A content sigh escapes my chest.

The sofa feels silky against my skin. I imagine myself naked, waiting for Cash to get back. My body begins to tingle, urging me to stop dreaming and start doing. While watching a movie might sound like a great way to spend the evening, engaging in some sexy activity with Cash is the more tempting option.

"Having fun without me?" A low voice says—too low, too close.

My eyes snap open.

Cash is standing at the foot of the sofa, his shirt unbuttoned, revealing rows and rows of hard muscles. My tongue flicks across my suddenly parched lips as my gaze roams over his body, drinking him in. He's carrying a tray while balancing on one crutch, which is amazing.

I want to comment on it, but decide not to because I don't want to make a big deal out of it and hinder his progress. I want him to act on his instincts, listen to his body, and just keep pushing himself without overthinking it.

I crane my neck, but before I can glimpse what's on the tray, he raises it higher, out of my view.

His eyes are hooded, dark with desire.

"What are you doing?" I ask, breathless.

"I'm working on the setting." He jiggles a pair of handcuffs. "You're going to be tied to my bedpost."

"I don't see a bedpost." He points at what looks like two silver hooks on either side of me. "Oh." The image of me naked, my thighs spread open for him, enters my mind and my core pulses to life as lust courses through my body.

"Want to know what happens next?" Under heavy lids, his eyes glow with an insatiable hunger for me. "I'll lick every part of your body until you're begging me to take you. And then I'll make you fall in love with me."

"I'm already in love with you, Cash. Remember?" I squeeze my hands under my shirt and pull it over my head, ready to give him what he wants.

Slowly, he begins to peel off his clothes, revealing his ripped torso and strong shoulders. As I watch his jeans and pants drop to the floor, I realize I'm not just in love with him. I'm falling for him over and over again.

Slowly, I get up from the sofa and begin to take

my clothes off, my body burning under his hooded gaze.

CHAPTER
TWENTY-FOUR

ERIN

I DON'T KNOW what I'm doing, only that I can't stop myself.

Heat at the prospect of getting intimate with him courses through me. As I slowly begin to undress, the memory of Sam is forgotten, replaced with a need to succumb to the lust that seems to consume me whenever I'm in Cash's presence.

I'm addicted to his kisses, his touch, his smile. There's something about his soft, deep voice that draws me to him, and then there's the curiosity whether he'll make our next sex session as good as the ones before.

My pulse thuds so hard I can barely breathe. Peeling my clothes off seems to take forever. When

I'm finally standing before him naked in all my glory, I sit on the edge of the sofa and motion for him to come closer.

He's already hard, his shaft thick and long, gleaming with a drop of moisture. Suddenly, I want to taste him the way he's tasted me.

Cash hesitates, but eventually does as I instruct. I place my hands on his hips and peer up into his green eyes a moment before I lower my mouth and suck him between my lips. He wraps his hand around the back of my head, but doesn't force himself deeper into my mouth.

I run my fingers up and down his slick shaft and lean in, trailing my tongue along the tip. He tastes just I imagined it—masculine and heady. I glide him back into my mouth as far as I can, my lips tightening to give him more friction.

"Erin." He sucks in his breath and lets out an appreciative groan.

As I start to rock back and forth in a slow rhythm, his groans intensify. He's so big and hard, a trembling mass of tension, that it's only a matter of time until he comes.

I let my tongue swirl again before sucking hard, alternating between teasing and guiding his hips to thrust into my mouth. He grips my head and lets out another groan, but instead of coming, he pulls out, his dick slick and glistening with lust.

"Did I do something—" I start when he flips me onto my stomach, cutting me off. A soft shriek escapes my lips as he pushes me back onto the sofa.

"What are you doing?" I turn to regard him and notice his green eyes are dark and hooded with lust. He's so turned on that his cock's huge, and dangerously close to my entrance. Instant moisture pools between my legs, readying me for what I desperately want.

"I don't want to see you naked on your knees. I want to be inside you, and find out if you're as sweet and delicious as you look like," Cash growls.

"Then do it now." I make eye contact and gasp as she presses his cock against me, rubbing his length from my clit to my core. His hands settle on my hips, drawing me closer to him, our bodies in perfect alignment.

He peers at me with concern. "You sure?"

I nod, and he presses his length against my pussy, rubbing it up and down against my clit, robbing me of my senses.

"Oh, that's good," I prompt, eager to get started.

"Is your pussy wet enough for me?" he asks in that deep rumble of his. "Let's find out."

Without waiting for my reply, he raises my hips a little higher, splaying me open before him. And then he's inside me, stretching me the way I've never been stretched before.

I throw my head back and let out a whimper. It doesn't hurt, but the sensation consumes me nonetheless. The sense of fullness is robbing me of all senses.

"More. Take me. Own me. Never let me wait." I moan and lean back, my walls clenching to get more of him inside me. Desire thrums like the string of a guitar, pulsing and vibrating through my entire body.

"I don't intend to, sweetheart. You are going to be mine...and mine alone." For a while, he keeps still inside me as I get used to his size, but his fingers are playing with my clit, stroking, putting pressure, preparing me for what's to come. I moan with pleasure and move my hips some more, silently urging him on because I can't take the wait.

I have to have him now.

"Cash, please," I beg when I feel I can't take his torture any longer.

"Relax, baby," he whispers, and I know that the safest place is here—with him.

Finally, his length thrusts into me, moving slowly

until my moisture begins to ease the way. With each stroke I can feel my orgasm building, taking me to the brink of something powerful and amazing. My internal muscles begin to contract around him. And when he presses his fingers to my clit, the pressure is so strong it sends me over the edge.

And I take him with me, the heat of his release so strong it brings on another wave.

His hands let go of me and he collapses onto the sofa, drawing me to his chest. I snuggle against him, spent, my breathing short and labored as our hearts beat together.

***

I wake up, confused, unsure of where I am. The walls are colored in a soft blue hue. My first impression is that it's still early morning, and the sun hasn't broken through the thick curtain of last night's clouds. And then I realize we're still in Cash's home cinema and there are no windows to let in the glorious morning rays.

My cell phone shows it's already past 10 a.m.

I get up to gather my scattered clothes and notice the empty bottle and wine glasses littering the table. Some of the pillows are piled up in a telltale arrangement. My cheeks warm up as I remember Cash's weight pinning me against them to ride me hard.

By the way, where is he?

There's no sign of him. No note. Nothing.

Which can only mean he's making breakfast.

I slip into last night's clothes and make my way upstairs. The door's open. On a hunch, I step into Cash's bedroom and peek into his walk-in closet. Some of the hangars hang empty on the rack. The space where I swear I saw a brown suitcase is empty, too.

Obviously, I'm not familiar with the contents of his closet, but I'm pretty sure Cash packed up a few things.

My heart drops.

Swallowing the bitter acid rising in my throat, I check his bathroom and find it meticulously clean, but that's not what worries me.

His toothbrush is missing.

Unease washes over me, followed by fury.

He wouldn't just up and leave without telling me, would he?

Just because some clothes, his suitcase, and toothbrush are missing doesn't mean he's left. Right?

"Cash," I call out and get no answer.

I head for the kitchen, half expecting to find him there, wearing nothing but a cocky smile. Or maybe we have a visitor, and he hasn't heard me calling.

But the kitchen is empty, too. There's no brewed coffee, no lingering smell of bacon and eggs. Not even the smell of his aftershave.

"Cash," I call out again, even though I know better than to expect an answer.

More acid rises in my throat, choking me. Where the hell is he?

That's when I spy Margaret through the window. My heart's beating fast as I dash outside.

She greets me with a smile. "Erin, how are you?"

"Where's Cash?" I ask, ignoring her question, my voice shaking with anger. I'm so livid I don't mind that my hair's a mess and my clothes are disheveled.

"Oh dear." She regards me for a few long moments, her gaze prodding but not judging. "Let's go inside. I'll make you some tea."

I fold my arms over my chest, not wanting to sound rude, but I can't help myself. "I don't need tea. I need to know where Cash is right now."

"He left early this morning. My husband drove him to the airport."

"Airport? Why would he..." Hundreds of thoughts

begin to race through my mind. Why didn't he wake me up? Why didn't he tell me that he needed to leave? Why didn't he bother leaving a note? I push them all to the back of my mind to focus on the conversation. "Did he say where he was going?"

"Only that it was business related and important."

I nod. What could possibly be so important that he left without waking me?

Surely if it were an emergency, he would have told me.

"When did he ask you to take him to the airport?"

Her warm eyes meet mine, hesitating. But why? She's considering whether to lie, but she won't. I know it. "He asked us yesterday. He wanted to be picked up at six sharp."

"Right. Of course." I storm inside, leaving Margaret staring after me. Once I've reached my bedroom, I grab my phone. My finger hovers over the touchscreen.

I have to call Shannon. But what should I tell her? That Cash has just disappeared on me? I sink down onto my bed, my hands shaking.

Cash is an adult. He doesn't have to tell me a damn thing. I have no right to inquire where he is.

Even though he told me that he loved me, we're

not in a relationship.

Absentmindedly, I swipe my finger over the screen. I'm on the way back to the kitchen when it lights with three texts, all from him.

I stop mid-stride.

My heart thuds as I read the first text.

Cash: Business emergency. Had to take the first plane.

I frown. That's a lie given that he knew he had to leave and could have told me last night.

I move on the second text.

Cash: Won't be back before the weekend. Please water the plants.

My frown deepens. Please water the plants? What the fuck?

The last message reads:

Cash: Enjoy your week off. I don't know when I'll be back.

That's it? No more info? And why the formality?

We fucked a few hours ago, and he treats me like I'm a mere employee.

The arrogant SOB.

I read the text messages over and over again, trying to make sense of them. But I don't understand what's going on. I don't understand why he's being the way he is.

I should be grateful that he texted at all, but all those weeks together, his declaration of love and him telling me that I was important to him, they all made me feel like something magical was happening between us.

Clearly, I was wrong.

Maybe he wanted me to sleep in, get some rest. But why ask Margaret's husband to drive him to the airport knowing I would have wanted to drive him?

Unless he thought I might ask questions. Questions he didn't want to answer.

But why?

My heart skips a beat, then another. Without thinking, I start to type, my anger flaring up again.

Me: Why didn't you tell me you needed to leave? I could have driven you to the airport.

I wait a few minutes. When it's clear he has

decided to ignore me, I draft another text.

Me: Where are you? Please call me as soon as you can. I'm worried. Tell me what's going on.

Half an hour later, there's still no reply, no sign he's even read my messages. With every passing hour I get more anxious, unable to do anything but stare at the cell phone in my hand. I'm so anguished that I brush off Margaret as she offers to take me shopping.

As if Cash's sudden aloofness isn't bad enough, my sister texts me, forcing me to lie.

Debra: Guess what? I got the promotion. How was your week?

Me: Congrats. You deserve it. I had a great time. Gotta get to work. Kiss the kids for me.

I finish typing up a response to Debra's text and then switch off my phone. A great time is an understatement. I've had a fantastic time. Everyone's been welcoming, showing me how much they appreciate my work. Such a shame Cash doesn't feel the same way.

Everything was perfect...until now.

Until Cash decided to leave without a word, as if I'm some acquaintance, his therapist, a friend, nothing more than a fuck buddy.

I shake my head grimly to fight off the moisture gathering in my eyes. I'm not crying because I've just realized he never trusted me; I'm crying because of the way he's made me feel.

I feel dirty, used, taken for granted.

Sleeping with him was a mistake.

I should never have believed his promises because they were worthless.

New fact I've just found out about my new patient: Cash Boyd likes to waste no opportunity making it clear that I'm nothing to him.

CHAPTER TWENTY-FIVE

CASH

THERE'S A SAYING in sports, which says you're only as good as your reputation. Or your win. Or a gold medal. Or whatever you're fighting for. The same saying can be applied in business.

The deal is done. Dillinger's mine. It's been a long two days of hard bargaining and a lot of cash exchanging hands, the process both tiring and bringing me relief because I can finally close this chapter of my life.

That's right, I'm done with it because there's something else in my life now that brings me even more fulfillment.

It started out as a crazy thought, an idea. After Erin mentioned that she hated the idea of bulls being tortured, it was a done deal to me.

I had to have him.

There was no way I'd let an invincible bull like Dillinger be put down just because he had become replaceable. He almost killed me, yes, but he also helped me meet Erin, and for that I'll always be grateful.

As I pull up to the house, I can't wait to see my woman. I should have called Erin, talked to her, told her about my plans, but I needed to find closure myself, on my terms.

Buying Dillinger was all the closure I needed, the final step to put my past behind me.

It's early morning, the sun still low on the horizon.

The car comes to a screeching halt in the driveway. I barely remember to slam the door before I'm up the stairs and heading into the hallway.

The house is eerily quiet, but the female touch is everywhere. In the vases with wildflowers and the cushions that are adorning the leather sofas.

My woman's touch.

I smile as I realize just how much I've grown to love having Erin's presence around me, how much peace her words of encouragement and her calm nature have brought me. Her touch and smile have made a difference in my life.

I missed her during my two-day absence.

Two whole days wasted without her.

My body missed her. My heart was empty without her.

Erin has become my life.

It took me a while to realize that the feelings I have for her won't pass, and now I can only hope that she feels the same way about me. The thought of asking her to move in with me, not just as my therapist, but as my girlfriend, fills me with excitement.

Dillinger's made me realize life's too short to let something good pass. She's that something good, that special someone who's made me want to leave my past behind and be excited about the future.

I can't wait to share my victory with her and then celebrate together in my bed, where I intend to keep her for the rest of our existence.

Or as long as our love will last.

"Erin," I call out impatiently, burying my hand in my pocket, fingering the other thing I acquired in the city.

She's not answering, but she can't be far. I search the kitchen and the living room, then move down the hall, checking out my bedroom first because that's where I expect to find her.

Sleeping in our bed, the sheets barely covering her delicious body.

Instead, strange noises carry over from her bedroom. Noises that sound like—

Frowning, I stop dead in the doorway, taking in the picture before me.

Erin's leaning over her suitcase, stuffing everything in haphazardly, her beautiful face determined and furious.

Fuck, she's packing again.

What the—

"What are you doing?"

Slowly, she turns to look at me, her face a mask of fury, her marvelous eyes shooting bolts of lightning. My frown deepens.

What the fuck did I do this time?

"You went to Paeroa." It's not a question; it's a statement.

Shit.

She knows, and judging from the way her voice is shaking with anger, her entire body trembling, I'm in big trouble.

CHAPTER TWENTY-SIX

ERIN

"DO YOU HAVE any idea how much pain you've caused me?" My voice is shaking as I stare at Cash, taking in the dark shadows around his eyes and the tired expression on his face.

"It wasn't my intention," he says softly.

"It wasn't?" I laugh. "You're a prick. After pouring my heart out to you, after everything we've fought for, getting you as far as possible in such a short time, you went to Paeroa. You said you'd never risk your life again, and yet—" I shrug, fighting for words. That he went to a bull riding event shouldn't be a big deal. But it is. None of the accidents he had ever stopped him from pursuing this madness of his. I harbor no false hope that this time things are different.

"Erin." Cash touches my arm gently. I pull back, frustrated, furious, hurt.

"Sleeping with you was a mistake. Do you realize how you've just made me feel? Dirty, used, like the last few weeks were just a big joke to you." I pause to regard him for a moment. He remains quiet, his eyes taking me in, his expression betraying no emotion. "I thought we had something, and then you up and left, and betrayed the trust I put in you."

I start to squeeze more clothes into my suitcase.

"I won't let you leave," Cash says with enough determination to make me look up from my task.

"Why? Because you're used to the world catering to your every whim? Big newsflash. You don't own me."

"I love you."

I blink, confused. "What?"

"You heard me." He's reached me in two long strides and sinks onto the bed, bringing his face close to me. "I'm sorry, but I'm not sorry that I can't let you go. You're far too important to me."

I scoff, fighting the urge to roll my eyes. "Obviously not important enough that you wouldn't betray my trust."

"I never betrayed your trust, Erin," Cash says. "I

promised that I would never ride, and I haven't."

"I don't believe you." I cross my arms over my chest as I try to read his expression. He looks honest, his words ringing with truth, but maybe he's just a good liar. "Why did you go to Paeroa, then?"

"To buy Dillinger."

I stare at him for a few seconds. His words echo in my mind, but I can't quite grasp their meaning...or make sense of them.

"To do what?"

"To buy the bull." Cash laughs at my shocked expression. "My guys are readying his new home this instant."

"Why would anyone want to buy a bull if they're not planning on riding it?"

"In the beginning, I planned on getting back in the saddle. But then you had that accident, and it got me thinking. I don't want to lose you, but more than that, I want to live. I want to see where this relationship might take us. And then a friend called to tell me that Dillinger was going to be euthanized because he's become too uncontrollable and I knew I had to save him."

"You never rode?"

Cash shakes his head, and a little smile lights up his eyes. "No."

"You sure?"

"I promised I wouldn't."

My doubts slowly begin to melt away. I want to throw myself into his arms, thankful that he didn't risk his life. But I hold back because he still hasn't answered all my questions.

"Why?" I ask warily.

"Why what?"

"Why would you buy him?"

Cash sighs, and for a moment it feels as though even he doesn't know the answer to my question. "Dillinger's cost me a lot of money. It might not sound like a good investment, but I think I know the right people to tame him. And even if he won't be tamed, he sort of saved my life, not literally speaking. I owe him that, in a twisted kind of way."

"But..." I shake my head. "He almost killed you."

"Yes, but he was an unwilling participant in the matter. No one gave him a choice. Besides, the way I see it, without Dillinger I might never have met you." He pulls me onto the bed. I settle beside him, my hands instinctively touching the gruff on his cheeks. "You know what? I actually asked him if he wanted to spend the rest of his life in Madison Creek, even though it can be quite boring? I mean, nothing ever happens."

"And what did he say?"

"He said you better make my stay worth it." He pulls himself on top of me, his weight pinning me down. I wrap my legs around him, my core tingling with anticipation. "I wouldn't think of disappointing you, Erin. I made a promise to you, and I'm going to honor it. Unless..." He places a soft kiss on my lips. "Unless you break up with me."

"Break up with you?" He can't be serious. I laugh at his ridiculous statement. "Even if I wanted you, you wouldn't let me leave. Remember?"

"I'm glad we've established that." His lips brush my cheeks, trailing down my neck, my collarbone. I grind my hips against his and find him rock hard. "Do you want to leave?"

Do I want to leave?

Hell, no. I want to stay for as long as I can.

For as long as this lasts. But what is *this*?

"I don't understand," I whisper. "When you say 'break up with you,' are you talking about a therapist patient kind of relationship or—"

"Don't pretend you don't know what I'm talking about, Erin. My family knows. My friends do. Maybe even the whole town."

"Know what?"

"That I'm fucking you. I told my Dad at some

point. Strangely, he had changed his mind and thought it was a good thing. By now, everyone knows we're an item."

"You told your dad?" I'm so mortified I could crawl under a rock. "But nobody's mentioned anything."

"Because I asked them not to. What?" He laughs at my horrified expression. "There's no such thing as a secret in my family. You might as well just spill it out because once they're done with you, they'll know all the skeletons you're hiding in the closet and then some."

I short laugh escapes my throat. "Nice way of talking about your family." I'm mortified, but at the same time, I feel giddy beyond control. The whole world knows about us. It's official. There's no going back. "Aren't you supposed to ask me first whether I was okay with it?"

His eyes glint with mischief. "I asked you…in your sleep. You said yes."

"You can't be serious."

"I am." He sounds so grave, my smile slowly vanishes.

Something's wrong.

In a good way, but still wrong.

"Why are you smiling?" I ask warily.

He squeezes his hand inside his pocket to retrieve his phone. "I thought you might not believe me, so I recorded you."

He scrolls through his apps and then hands me his cell, pressing play.

CHAPTER
TWENTY-SEVEN

ERIN

THIS MUST BE the biggest, most ridiculous and embarrassing moment of my life. The one that is surely going to haunt me for as long as I exist.

I stare at the screen and inwardly cringe, the words barely squeezing past my lips. "When did you record this?"

"Three weeks ago," Cash says with an annoying grin. "It gets really good. Just wait for it."

Did he just say 'weeks?'

I fight the urge to cover my eyes as I take in the way I cling to his chest, my eyes glazed over like I'm drunk.

But I'm not drunk.

I'm still asleep with my eyes open. He's standing

next to me, his arm raised to record us on his phone. Judging from the way his cell phone shakes a few times, he's having the laugh of his life.

"Now, Erin, please repeat what you just asked me." Cash briefly zooms in on himself, and I catch his big ass grin for a second before I'm back in the video.

"Cash," I say. "You're easily the hottest guy I've ever met in my life."

Oh, hell no! I didn't admit that he's the hottest guy I've ever met within days of sleeping with him.

I'm surprised he hasn't run for the hills yet.

"And?" Cash prompts in the video, drawing out the word.

"It's seriously hard to stay away from you, which is why I'm proposing."

Looking at the camera again, he grins. I almost expect him to make the thumbs-up sign, but he doesn't. "You're proposing? To *me*?"

Video me starts to nod eagerly. "Oh yeah. Big time."

What the heck?

I stop the video. My whole body's burning from sheer mortification. Closing my eyes, I force slow breaths into my lungs, but no oxygen reaches my brain.

"Please don't tell me I proposed to you," I whisper.

"You did," Cash says. "That took guts."

I shake my head. "I must have been drunk. Or something hit me over the head. Because there's absolutely no other reasonable explanation for it."

"Actually, you weren't any of those things. I believe the correct term is sleep walking. Now, watch this. This is my favorite part." He resumes playing the video, and like someone strapped to a chair, with their eyes forced wide open, I'm forced to watch myself rambling on with excitement.

"They call it lovestruck. I was struck by a tractor, but I never got the love. Why waste time waiting, Cash? I want to marry you and have your babies. And have sex every day."

"My babies?" Cash is laughing in the video. "Not bad. How many exactly are we talking about? Just asking to make sure we have enough room in the house."

My cheeks begin to burn as I catch the happy glow on my face. "Four? Five? I would want to name them Josh, Jenny, Maggie, Becks."

I sound as though I've given this plenty of thought.

"You would be happy living here with me?" Cash

asks in the video.

"Yeah. As long as we get to have sex every day. Love struck, remember?" I nod like a complete idiot. "I can't imagine being anywhere else but here, with you."

"And do you know who I am?" Cash asks, zooming closer.

"Of course, I know who you are, Cash. When are we getting married?"

The footage ends.

I don't even dare to look at him. After watching this, I don't know how I'll ever be able to face him again, talk to him, even manage to be in his presence without the picture of me revealing my plans to have his children entering my mind.

Embarrassment can't even begin to describe what I'm feeling.

As a child and teen, I used to sleepwalk, but I thought I had grown out of it like a kid grows out of a pair of shoes. I thought I had left it all behind, but apparently not.

"You should have shown me the video straight away."

"I wanted to save it for a special occasion," Cash says.

"I don't know what to say," I mutter. "Of course I

didn't mean any of it."

"So you say, but your unconscious knows better."

I lift my gaze to regard him. "Yes, but that doesn't mean I really want us to get married. This…" I point to the phone. "I wasn't supposed to say it like that."

Cash smiles, and a strange glint appears in his eyes.

"What?" I prompt.

"Aren't you going to ask me what I replied to your question?"

Do I even want to know?

I notice the way he blinks.

I notice the way his lips quirk.

All in slow motion.

"What did you say?" I whisper.

"I said proposing is a guy's job." He reaches into his pocket and pulls out a box. My eyes meet his, and for a moment I forget to breathe.

Surely…it can't be what I think—no, make that hope—it is…

Cash opens the box, revealing a ring.

"I want to marry you, Erin," he says softly. "But for different reasons than you want to marry me. Even though I love your body and can't wait to have sex every single day, I also love you. I told you this before, and I intend to tell you every single day for the rest of our lives." He pauses to take my hand in his. "I love you for all the right reasons. While I don't expect you to marry me now, I want you to be mine someday. So will you, Erin Stone, do me the honor and marry me when the time is right? When you don't think we're being too rash, going too fast, and the idea seems less crazy?"

"Wow." My cheeks are hurting from so much smiling, and I can barely pry my gaze off the beautiful halo diamond ring. "Wow."

I finally look up into Cash's green eyes, and that's when my tears start to fall like tiny rivulets of happiness.

This moment is so unlike any other I've ever experienced. It's so crazy and unreal that it really suits Cash. I wouldn't have expected anything else from him.

Laughing through my tears, I nod.

"Yes," I whisper. "Yes. I'd love to."

EPILOGUE

Ten months later

They call it lovestruck. I was struck by a tractor, but I never got the love.

THE FOOTAGE SEEMS to be running on a loop. At least it feels that way. It's probably been seen by every single one of our hundreds of guests. Everyone's here—Cash's dad, his brothers, his relatives, all his friends, every face I've seen in town. Everyone's laughing and having a great time while I keep cringing and blushing. But even I have to admit that my sleepwalking is hilarious.

I look like I'm completely out of my mind proposing to Cash weeks after meeting him.

Even my mom can't help herself divulging a few embarrassing stories about my past, recalling all the stupid things I used to do while sleepwalking, which, by the way, is said to be stress related and no doctor can cure.

I cringe some more and then give up kicking her leg under the table. I mean, what's the point? She doesn't seem to want to stop embarrassing me anytime soon, so I might as well give up.

Having a whole town knowing your private business and then some doesn't come naturally to me, but like Cash once said, "You might as well just spill it out." And then he said something about everyone being so far up your ass you can't ever get rid of them, and went on to compare them with IBS. The analogy was so inappropriate I almost fainted from laughter.

I can only hope my embarrassing proposal to Cash won't be uploaded on Youtube. If that happens, I'll have to wear a paper bag over my head for the rest of my life.

As it turns out, I've sleepwalked a few more times since my unexpected proposal. Cash has made it a habit of conversing with me whenever it happens, if only to listen to the nonsensical things I say. According to him, he's only making sure I don't do something stupid and hurt myself, but I know better.

Secretly, he's getting a good laugh out of it.

I'm such an open book, even in my sleep. I practically pour my whole self out to him, reveal my secret wishes, plans, and dreams while not remembering a thing.

Reminder for the future: Never deliberately ignore your thoughts and feelings because they'll come back to bite you sooner or later.

They have a way to turn up when you least expect them. In my case, denying my feelings for Cash only made me want him more and fall for him harder.

My little sleepwalking secret isn't a secret anymore, but Cash seems to love this side of me. Holding the mic, that's what he tells our guests. That I'm perfect for him. That I helped him find his way out of a dark place.

That I was the one who changed him.

During his speech, Cash is standing without the need for crutches. He tossed those out ages ago. Even though he's regained full mobility, he's kept true to his word and riding is now a thing of the past, for which everyone's grateful.

His green eyes remain fixed on me, as though the world as we know it has ceased to exist and we're the only people left in the world.

With tears in my eyes, I stare at the man I've married, marveling at his beauty, his perfection, the amazing feelings he evokes in me.

"I love you," I whisper so low he can't possibly have heard me through the crowd, but it doesn't matter. I let him know every day in as many ways as I can. Because once you find 'the one' don't ever let him forget just how much he means to you.

"May I have this dance, Mrs. Boyd?" Cash asks, reaching for me.

"I'd love that, Mr. Boyd." I wrap my arms around his neck, clasping my fingers at the nape of it. "Any chance you're ever going to delete the video?" I whisper in his ear as we slowly begin to sway with the music, our bodies in perfect tune.

"That's not ever going to happen. I've already uploaded it on the cloud. And what's on the cloud, is forever."

I sigh in mock exasperation. "You can't blame a girl for trying."

The romantic music changes into some fast tune, and Cash starts to spin me around, just like we've practiced. He's in such a great shape now, I can barely keep up with him.

The guy isn't just a sex god, he can also move like one.

"Did you already know you wanted to marry me when you gave me that necklace?" I force him to slow down so I can catch my breath.

"The thought occurred to me the first moment you knocked the air out of me, which was the day we met."

I laugh until I catch his serious expression. "You're lying. There's absolutely no way you thought about marrying me within a few minutes of meeting me."

"I did." He nods. "I thought, 'damn, if she were my wife, I'd spank her ass and spank it good.'" It was only a thought, obviously, but it paved the way. After that, I tried to get rid of you because I thought you couldn't possibly be into a guy who couldn't even walk. That's why I wanted to fire you."

I roll my eyes playfully. "Let's be honest. You bribed and fired everyone."

"Yes, but you were persistent, stubborn, and bossy, which ticked me off so bad it was either spank you or marry you."

"My hard work's paid off." I let him spin me around one last time. "I can only hope you'll keep your promise about bull riding because I don't ever want to have to worry about your life. I couldn't bear losing you."

"I will. But what about skydiving?"

I shake my head. "No."

"Boxing?"

"Absolutely not, Cash."

"And what if I need to test drive Dillinger's future offspring?"

"Seriously?" I glare at him even though I know he's only joking. "Forget it."

"What about trying out some weird sex positions?"

"Now we're talking." I lock my arms behind his head and pull him closer. "And what about taking me on a ride on your new motorcycle?"

"It's not a motorcycle," I repeat my father's words. "It's a Harley Davidson."

"Of course. Let's go then."

"Now?"

"Now. Let's keep it brief. Maybe an hour. No one will notice our absence." My core begins to tingle at the prospect of Cash taking me to a secluded spot, and fucking me with my bridal gown gathered around my hips. The gown is huge with a corset that's squeezing my lungs, but we'll make it work.

His brows shoot up. "An hour? I only need thirty minutes."

"Why thirty?"

"To make you come at least twice." He winks, and a naughty glint appears in his eyes. "Let's go. There's still plenty of work lined ahead of us. I have to put my babies in you. Remember?"

"You didn't just say that out loud for the whole world to hear," I say, mortified. I'm pretty sure everyone around us has heard him. "Besides, I'm not squeezing four kids out of me. I'm not ready yet."

"*Yet*, sweetheart. The keyword is *yet*. But someday...probably very soon." He kisses me softly on the lips. "I'm wild for you, Erin Stone. As long as I breathe, I'll make you happy, as long as you promise you'll always be mine."

I look into his beautiful green eyes.

His eyes shimmer, piercing into my heart, seeking my soul.

He's beautiful.

Breathtaking.

Unforgettable.

And so deliciously close he's stealing my breath away.

"I promise," I whisper with two tears of happiness trickling down my cheeks. "I promise I'll always be yours."

"Always?"

"Always." Closing my eyes, I press my mouth against his, bathing in the sea of emotions, forgetting the world around us, thanking my lucky stars, and all the people in his life who've brought us together.

Even Dillinger, in a twisted kind of way.

"I'll never let you go," Cash whispers in my ear.

"Is that a promise or a threat?"

"Both." Cash smiles before he leans in to kiss me again, his breath making me weak.

In that instant, I know he'll never let me down.

Cash is like my very own ocean—pretty on the surface, but once I dived deeper I started to see the beautiful parts of him no one had ever seen before. Those are the parts I fell in love with.

Love doesn't change you. It brings out the best in you. It makes you want to be the person you're inside. It's brought out the real Cash who's so much more amazing than the jerk who couldn't wait to get me in his bed.

I never had to ask Cash to change for me. The perfect man was there all along, hiding behind a mountain of guilt and self-doubt as wide as the sky.

I came to Montana on a mission, and I never left.

Some things are just meant to be. Cash and I are one of them.

----THE END----

Want to read more about the Boyd brothers, Kellan, Cash and Ryder?

Meet Ryder Boyd in my next standalone:

Ryder Boyd ➡ **NO ONE LIKE YOU**

In the meantime, check out Kellan Boyd's story in

BEAUTIFUL DISTRACTION

Don't miss their release. Subscribe to the J.C. Reed Mailing List to be notified on release day:
http://www.jcreedauthor.com/mailinglist

Watch out for

NO ONE LIKE YOU

(A STANDALONE NOVEL)

BY J.C. REED

COMING February 2017

ACKNOWLEDGMENTS

My first and foremost thanks goes out to my readers, wherever you are. This book wouldn't exist without your support. Thank you.

Thank you also to my awesome editors, Kim and Elaine, for always going above and beyond the call of duty.

Huge thank you to my very talented cover artist. Your covers always make me blush. A big thank you from the bottom of my heart goes to all the bloggers who helped me spread the word. You didn't have to, and yet, you take the time "to read and review, and to help me get this book out there.

I also want to thank my family for their continued support. For my dear friend Fancy. This book would not exist without your support. I wish you would still be part of this journey. You will be missed.

And finally, I thank the Lord for gifting me the opportunity to write my stories and share them with my wonderful readers.

Thank you!

Jessica

ABOUT THE AUTHOR

J.C. Reed is the multiple New York Times, Wall Street Journal and USA Today bestselling author of the SURRENDER YOUR LOVE series and BEAUTIFUL DISTRACTION. She writes steamy contemporary romance and mystery with alpha males who'll melt your panties.

https://www.facebook.com/AuthorJCReed

http://www.jcreedauthor.com

BOOKS BY J.C. REED:

SURRENDER YOUR LOVE TRILOGY

SURRENDER YOUR LOVE
CONQUER YOUR LOVE
TREASURE YOUR LOVE

NO EXCEPTIONS SERIES

THE LOVER'S SECRET
THE LOVER'S GAME
THE LOVER'S PROMISE
THE LOVER'S SURRENDER

Made in the USA
Middletown, DE
08 September 2017